THE
One-Night
STAND

THE
One-Night
STAND

ELIZABETH HAYLEY

WATERHOUSE PRESS

*To Jack and Rose, for teaching us how a
one-night stand shouldn't end. #neverletgo*

P.S. We would've made room for you on that door, Jack.

CHAPTER ONE

RACHEL

Rachel hustled through the newsroom, her brown hair bouncing against her shoulders as her mind whirled with all the different things her boss, Rick Hartnett, might want to talk to her about. None of them were good.

She'd been a reporter with all access sports magazine practically since she'd graduated college, but as she let her eyes roam around the room, she noticed the thrill wasn't as strong as it used to be. It wasn't that she didn't like her job or had much of a desire to move on to a different publication. Rather, it was that she felt stagnant. Every day there was a reminder that she hadn't reached the kind of success she'd hoped she would have after nearly a decade in the industry.

Reaching the door of Rick's office, she gave it a few raps. "You wanted to see me?" she asked after he looked up from his computer.

"Yeah," he replied, gesturing to the chair on the other side of his desk. Though *All Access Sports* was on the twenty-second floor of a building that was less than twenty years old, their space was anything but sleek. Stacks of old newspapers and magazines littered Rick's floor, and Rachel had to step around them to make it to the chair.

Rachel took a seat without closing the door, since Rick always preferred it stay open. She and Rick engaged in some sort of odd staring contest before he finally picked up the next edition of their print magazine and dropped it on the desk in front of her.

"You want to tell me why you don't have an article in there?"

No, actually she didn't want to tell him. "I didn't have anything solid to contribute."

Rick steepled his hands and let his chin rest atop them. "Hmm. That's interesting. Because when I looked into our budget analytics for last month, I see that you flew across the goddamn country to chase a story. But"—Rick slapped a finger onto the magazine—"I don't see a story."

"The lead didn't pan out."

"I didn't even approve that trip. How'd you get the go-ahead?"

Rachel shrugged in an overly casual way that was an attempt to pretend she wasn't about to get reamed out by her boss. And what was worse, she deserved it. "You weren't here when the story came up, so I asked Cal."

"You asked Cal, a junior editor with no actual authority, to make this decision?"

"Accounting thinks he has authority." It was not the brightest thing Rachel could have said in that moment, but it was at the very least true.

"But *you* know he doesn't. What was the story anyway? At our last pitch meeting, you said you were going to do a piece on the inflation of prices at ballparks. Pretty sure you didn't need to go to California for that."

Rachel looked down and studied her nails. She really needed to get a manicure. Her nail beds looked disastrous. "I heard some grumblings about the club, so I thought I'd check it out."

"Jesus Christ. Not this again."

Rachel let her hands drop into her lap. "Yes, this again. You know this is an ongoing investigation for me. If I can figure out the truth behind the rumors, it would make my whole career."

Sighing, Rick crossed his arms on his desk. "How long have you been looking into this club?"

"I'm not exactly sure," she hedged.

"Too long is the answer. You gotta drop this thing, Rach. If there were any truth to it, you'd have found out by now."

"Not necessarily. It's extremely exclusive. Only the best of the best get asked to join, so obviously they're going to be tight-lipped about it. I just have to find the right angle."

"Rachel."

"And I've found enough details to support its existence. I just don't have anything solid enough to base a story on."

"Rachel."

"But it's only a matter of time. The source in San Diego didn't pan out, but something else will. I just need to keep my ear to the ground."

"Rachel!" Rick yelled.

Taking a deep breath, she focused on him, even though she knew she wasn't going to like what he had to say.

"It's time to give it up. You're out there chasing a unicorn when there are more pressing things we need you to cover."

"It's not a unicorn. It's a Triple Crown winner."

"A hypothetical Triple Crown winner. That's not good enough to waste resources."

"I've spent years on this story. I can't—"

"You've spent years on it and have absolutely nothing to show for it. I'm sorry, but you need to drop it. We can't allocate any more resources toward it."

"I'll work it on my own time."

"We consider your time *our* resource. We pay you for it. We need your head to be in the game."

"You can't forbid me from working on something when I have nothing else going on."

"No. But I can fire you if you don't start providing usable material on a regular basis."

Rachel's eyes shot to his, hers widening in surprise. He'd never threatened to fire her before. Nothing even close.

Under her scrutiny, Rick's face softened. "Look, I'm not trying to scare you, but I do have to be honest. I can't have a reporter going rogue whenever she feels like it. We're a team here, and you used to be one of our most integral players. But it's like you've put yourself on the disabled list and refuse to do any more than take a few practice swings."

"That was . . . a really involved metaphor."

Rick rolled his eyes, but some of the good-natured vibes they normally had between them returned, which encouraged Rachel to be completely honest.

"This story is going to be epic, Rick. And it may not happen this month, or this year, but it's going to happen. And I'll be damned if it happens for someone else after I've spent so many years on it. I refuse to lose out because I was forced to give up."

"Listen. If something comes over the wire that even so much as hints at the club, you'll be the first one to know. But as far as using *All Access* time and resources to investigate it . . . Those days are over. When you're here, you're to work the assignments we give you. And for Christ's sake, next time you use company money to travel somewhere, you'd better go through the proper channels. I don't give a shit if you're riding a subway to Brooklyn. You clear it with me first."

Figuring this was the closest to a compromise as she was going to get, Rachel nodded. "Got it."

"Good. Now get out of here and pack."

Rachel startled. "Pack? I thought you'd just finished grounding me for the foreseeable future."

"Stop being a smartass, or I won't send you anywhere."

Rachel stood and smoothed out her black slacks. "Where am I going?"

Rick reached across his desk to retrieve the magazine. "The Super Bowl."

CHAPTER TWO

GABE

"Hey, Jace. If I kill someone, you'd come visit me in prison, wouldn't you?" Gabe sat back in his black leather chair and closed his eyes, squeezing the bridge of his nose. He felt a tension headache coming on, which would be a reprieve from the full-skull headaches he'd had almost daily since taking over the Players' Club.

Jace popped his head toward the office at the rear of the club. "That depends."

Gabe let his hand drop and sat up. "On what?"

"On if it was someone I liked or not."

"Oh, okay. We're all good then. Because there's no way you'd like this fucker."

"Which fucker are we talking about?"

Gabe took a deep breath and let it out slowly. "That asshole Cole Barnes. The guy who wants back in the club and isn't afraid to make threats to make it happen."

When Mike Tarino—the club's founder and original owner—died suddenly, Gabe felt like he'd be able to find a positive in the tragedy. He'd been thinking of retiring from baseball for some time, so when the opportunity to take over the club arose, he'd jumped on it. Losing Mike had hit Gabe harder than it had hit his best friends Jace and Ben, but he'd been determined to make Mike proud by running the club with the same love and dedication Mike had.

That was easier said than done. After Gabe had expressed an interest in the club to one of the managers, he'd been put in contact with a lawyer and gotten the ball rolling. A few other players had expressed the same interest, but as it turned out, Mike had left explicit instructions for the future of the club. And that had included a list of people Mike would have wanted to take over the place if anything happened to him.

Gabe had been floored to find out his name was at the top of the list. Though, in reality, he shouldn't have been too surprised. Mike and Gabe had talked at length about what Gabe wanted from his life after baseball: something that he could pour himself into, just like he'd done with baseball for most of his life. A new passion he could latch onto. Something that would revive the rut he felt he'd been in leading up to retirement.

But Gabe had been running the club for three months now, and he felt like he was drowning under the stress of the job. A fact Jace must have picked up on, since he'd sent Gabe a text an hour ago saying he was in the parking lot of the Players' Club and to let him the hell in. Jace had a couple of hours until he needed to be at his team's facility to run through some tape and said he was all Gabe's until then. Gabe would've kissed him if he hadn't thought Jace would punch him. Hard.

But now he looked like he wanted to punch Cole Barnes, which Gabe would ordinarily be down for, except Jace was a week away from playing in the Super Bowl, and Gabe didn't want the quarterback to fuck up his hand. "What threats? You didn't tell me he was making threats."

"Yes, I did," Gabe replied.

"No. You didn't."

"Oh." Gabe shrugged. "Well, I told someone. Maybe Ben." Jace glared at him, making Gabe laugh. He really couldn't ask for better friends. "He's not threatening to come after me with a baseball bat or anything. Just that if I don't reinstate him, he'll start talking about the club to whatever media outlet will listen."

"That'll make him real popular."

"He doesn't seem to care. Everyone hates him anyway. He's a prick." Gabe shuffled some papers around on his desk and tried to think of how best to deal with Cole.

When Gabe had taken over, the manager of the club had shared Mike's ban list with Gabe. There were only seven names on it—people Mike had to kick out of the club for a variety of infractions. Cole had been a notorious drug user at the end of his football career, and he'd brought that shit into the club and tried spreading it around.

Since Mike had not only been protecting the privacy of the professional athletes, who were members of the exclusive club that catered to the best in their respective leagues, but also their overall safety and well-being, he had a strict no drug policy. Cole had been shown the door immediately.

And because, Gabe assumed, Mike had connections that ran deep around the sports world, Cole hadn't fought to get back in. Until now. Gabe had no idea why being a member was so important to the guy, but it seemed to be Cole's mission now. But he was still bad news. There was no way Gabe was going to let him back in. He just needed to think of a way to keep the guy quiet.

If the media caught wind of the Players' Club, its entire purpose would be dismantled. Mike had opened the club so pro athletes could have somewhere to go where the media would never look for them. A place where they could unwind and be themselves. Gabe wasn't going to fuck up the safe-haven Mike had created. "I don't know. I can't think of any way to make him go away other than to have him whacked."

The corner of Jace's lips quirked up. "Been watching *Goodfellas* again?"

"*Sopranos*," Gabe answered.

"I can't believe Mike didn't leave any instructions on how to deal with these guys," Jace said.

"He probably assumed that anyone who took over the club would be able to handle it."

Jace's voice was softer when he responded. "True."

Gabe scrubbed his hands over his face. "I'm sure it'll all blow over. I'm stressed about it now, but if this guy's sat on info like this for this long, I don't think he'll actually do anything about it now. He's probably just making empty threats to try to get back in the club."

"You never know what people are capable of," Jace said, entering the office. "I wouldn't assume this dude'll just forget about it."

"So you think I should let him back in then?"

"No, not if Mike specifically said not to. And not if he's bad for the club."

Gabe thought for a moment, his options running through his mind like a movie reel. "Maybe I can make an example out of him and hang his severed arm in the hall like that one dude did to that other dude in that story we had to read in that freshman English class we had together."

Raising an eyebrow, Jace replied, "I should probably know what you're talking about, but despite your detailed description, I have no idea."

"Shut up. Yes, you do. It was that one with the monster."

"I got nothin'," Jace said.

"The title had something to do with a wolf or something, I think. And the dude fights the monster and the monster's mom."

Jace laughed. "*Beowulf?*"

"Yes!" Gabe shouted, pointing at Jace with excitement. He never would've remembered the title on his own. "I'll Beowulf the fucker. I'll go after Cole Barnes and his *mom*. That'll teach him to fuck with me."

"Sounds like a solid plan," Jace said. "Taking out both of them will definitely make your life stress-free."

"My thoughts exactly," Gabe said with a smile that actually wasn't forced. Even though he *was* concerned about Cole's intentions, Gabe did think things would work out for the best. "Anyway, thanks for your help, but I'm pretty sure you have better places to be."

Pulling his cell phone out of his pocket, Jace looked at the screen. "Nah. I got time."

"What are you even doing out there?" Gabe asked.

"Organizing boxes and shit. Straightening up. Whatever looks like it needs doing."

Gabe was quiet for a minute. "Thanks, man. I appreciate it." And he did. Gabe knew the place was in fairly good condition. He made sure of it. Jace wasn't there because Gabe was slacking. He was there because Gabe needed him to be. Needed another presence to keep him from losing his mind.

"It's no big deal. Aly has wedding magazines all over the

fucking place. I needed to get out of there."

Gabe's gaze jerked to Jace's. "Why is she looking at wedding magazines?" If this was Jace's way of telling Gabe he was engaged to his doctor girlfriend, Gabe was going to kick his ass.

Jace smirked. "Because subtlety isn't one of her strengths."

Relaxing back into his chair, Gabe smiled. "Well, if you get any ideas, just remember that I look great in red."

"I'll be sure to take your preferences into account when I plan my wedding," Jace said dryly.

"I appreciate it. I mean, ultimately I'll look good in anything. Probably better than you. You should maybe reconsider making me your best man." Gabe winked at Jace, doing what Gabe did best: using humor to mask the fact that he was fishing for information. Because if Jace was going to propose soon, Gabe wanted to know about it. And he also really did want to be the best man—he'd even share the honor with Ben. Gabe was magnanimous that way.

"I wasn't aware I'd named a best man, but thanks for letting me know."

Gabe scowled at his friend, who only laughed at him. "You're not going to be one of those losers who makes his brothers his best men out of some weird sense of family loyalty, are you? Because that seems really unfair."

Jace's brow furrowed. "Unfair to who?"

"Me," Gabe yelled, causing Jace to laugh again.

"Oh God forbid, I wouldn't want to be unfair to you."

"Good. I'm glad we got that settled."

Taking a couple paces toward Gabe, Jace plopped down into the chair on the other side of the desk. He rested his forearms on his knees, his hands clasped together, his face suddenly serious.

Gabe widened his eyes comically. "Holy shit! You're not proposing to me, are you? Because I gotta tell ya, even though I'm flattered, I can't do that to Aly."

"Shut up, smartass," Jace scolded, though the twitch of his lips betrayed his amusement. "I just wanted to make sure you knew that, if I do propose to Aly—"

"When. Don't give me that 'if' shit. We both know it's a 'when.'"

Jace rolled his eyes. "*When* I propose, there's no one else I'd rather have stand up there with me than you and Ben."

"Where's Aly going to stand?"

Picking up a stack of Post-Its, Jace threw them at Gabe. "Can you just let me be serious for a moment?"

If Gabe were being honest, he wasn't sure he could. It was either make a joke or cry like a sap. And since Jace wasn't likely to ever let him live the second one down, joking it would have to be. But as he looked at the sincerity in Jace's eyes, he couldn't keep it going.

"I'd be honored," Gabe said softly, all hint of laughter gone from his voice. The two men kept their eyes locked on one another for a heavy moment. Their gaze said what their mouths couldn't: how important their friendship was to each of them, how much they depended on one another, how they were more like brothers than buddies.

And then Jace nodded once and stood, effectively breaking their silent conversation. He stretched. "And maybe one day, you'll stop being a player and settle down so I can return the favor."

Gabe felt his face twist up. "Nah, man. Not me. I'm not the settling down type."

"That's what Ben and I said too," Jace said with a sly grin.

"Yeah, but you guys snagged the last two great girls on the planet. I'm shit out of luck." Gabe smiled, but there was truth hidden in the jest.

Gabe had dated—and fucked—his way through most of the greater Philadelphia area, and he'd yet to find anyone he felt he could go the distance with. Well, there was *one*, but that had been years ago in college, and Rachel hadn't given Gabe the chance to show her he was more than the player everyone claimed he was.

Though he couldn't say he blamed her. Gabe knew he was an acquired taste. He tended to be a little too much for the kind of girls someone would want to wife up. So he'd decided a long time ago that the single life suited him better. And he was okay with it. Really. He was.

"You'll see. It'll happen when you least expect it."

Since Gabe was never expecting it, using Jace's logic should've had Gabe married off by now, but he kept that thought to himself. "Whatever, Love Guru. Stop distracting me and go to practice. I've got big money on you winning the Super Bowl."

Jace winked as he walked toward the door. "Easiest money you've ever made, buddy."

"It better be," Gabe called after him as he left the office. Taking a minute to stare at the mountain of paperwork around him, Gabe sighed. When he'd left baseball, he thought his most grueling days were behind him. He'd never been more wrong.

CHAPTER THREE

GABE

Gabe looked up at the scoreboard and gripped Ben's arm. "Holy fuck. He's going to do it. He's really going to win the fucking Super Bowl."

Jace's teammates formed the victory formation as Jace took a knee with forty seconds left on the clock. His team, the Commanders, had just intercepted the ball at their own fifteen-yard-line from the Memphis Wolverines, who had been driving down the field like their asses were on fire. The Commanders were only up by three, so the interception had been a crucial play by the defense. Now all Jace had to do was kneel until the clock ran out.

Gabe couldn't believe it. His best friend was winning a goddamn Super Bowl. The atmosphere in the stadium was electric, and it pulsed through Gabe with every beat of his heart. *This* was the part of competing he missed. These moments that were few and far between but served to justify every sacrifice he'd ever made.

Jace kneeled for a final time, and Gabe launched himself at Ben, who clutched him in return. "Aren't you glad you told your coach to fuck off so you could be here?" Gabe asked Ben.

Ben laughed and pulled away from Gabe slightly, though they kept their arms around one another's shoulders. "Hell yeah."

Ben hadn't really told his coach to fuck off, but he had told him in no uncertain terms that he was going to Texas to see his best friend play in the Super Bowl no matter the consequence. Ben's coach told him that as long as he was present at the game the next day—and played as if he hadn't jetted off to Texas the day before—he wouldn't hold it against Ben. Which was why Ben and his girlfriend, Ryan, were flying back to Denver at four a.m. the next morning. But the truth was less fun, so Gabe was going to stick with his version of the story.

Gabe glanced across the box they were in to look at Aly, who was whooping and hollering like a madwoman. She was decked out in full Commander gear and seemed to think that Jace would be able to hear her if she yelled loudly enough.

Laughing, Gabe turned back to Ben, who was hugging Ryan to him. They were so cute it was sickening. "Get a room," he said because . . . well, what else would he say?

Ben flipped him off and went right back to cuddling.

"Why didn't you bring my lesbian best friend?" Gabe asked. "Then I would've had someone to make fun of you two with." Gabe was referring to Ryan's best friend, Camille, who Gabe adored, mostly because she was fun to argue with.

"We asked her, but then she heard you were coming," Ryan said with a shrug.

"That is a damn lie," Gabe argued. "She loves me. She's about two more months from going straight for me, you just watch."

Ryan and Ben burst out laughing, which made Gabe smile. In all honesty, he'd never met a woman more immune to his charms than Camille—and that included other lesbians. He could usually get anyone to at least flirt with him. But Camille had shut him down immediately upon meeting him. It was refreshing for Gabe to have someone be so utterly unimpressed by him.

"You two sound like you doubt me. I'll prove it," Gabe said as he pulled his phone out of his back pocket and sent Camille a text.

> *I'm at the game with Ben and Ryan, and they don't believe you'd have sex with me. Tell them how madly in love with me you are.*

Gabe said what he was typing out loud so Ben and Ryan would know what it said, and then pressed send. A reply came back almost instantly.

Who is this?

Ben read it over Gabe's shoulder and then collapsed into hysterics with Ryan.

> *Playing hard to get I see, I'm into that.*

You're into anything with a pulse.

Gabe laughed.

> *So you DO know who this is.*

Stop trying to sext with me and call me

when you get back to Philly. I have some
manual labor for you to do.

Gabe knew that was Camille-speak for asking him to hang out when he got back to the city.

Done. But I have one last
question for you.

What?

Your vibrator is named Gabe, isn't it?

Goodbye, Gabriel.

Gabe chuckled and pocketed his phone. He turned his attention to the chaos on the field. The Wolverines had finally left the field, and the league officials were starting to prepare for the presentation of the Vince Lombardi Trophy.

"You guys are lame for skipping out on the afterparty," Gabe said to Ben and Ryan.

"I told you we'd stop by for an hour or so," Ben said, sounding exasperated, probably because this was the eightieth time Gabe had razzed him about this.

Gabe looked at Ryan. "He used to be fun. You changed him." She'd actually changed him in all the best possible ways, but Gabe would keep that part to himself. And since Ryan chuckled in response, she clearly knew he was just giving her a hard time.

"I was never that much fun," Ben interjected.

"That's a very sad statement," Gabe said. "But also very

true. Who's going to babysit me? And get Aly when it's time to pump my stomach?"

"Guess you'll just have to be a big boy and not get out of hand," Ben answered.

"Being a big boy is overrated." As soon as the words were out of his mouth, Gabe knew he'd let them sound too honest.

Ben's eyes softened, and he looked like he wanted to ask about it, but Gabe knew he couldn't. Not with Ryan there. The Players' Club was a secret all members vowed to keep—even from loved ones. Gabe wasn't sure how the guys managed to keep it from the women in their lives. He figured it would be hard not being able to be honest about something like that. But the rules were in place for a reason, and it was a system that had been working for a long time. It wasn't going to change on his watch.

Time for a subject change. "Besides, I'm already big in all the ways that matter." Gabe winked at them, causing Ben to shake his head and Ryan to roll her eyes.

After that, the ceremony started. Jace won the MVP Award, which caused Aly to start bawling like a deranged baby. Gabe went over and slid an arm around her. "Our boy did good, didn't he?"

Aly rested her head on his shoulder. "He really did." They stood like that for the rest of the celebration—both of them reveling in seeing one of the people they loved most in the world fulfill one of his dreams.

★ ★ ★

Gabe was on his third gin and tonic and feeling pretty good. Despite owning a club, he didn't tend to drink much, so alcohol typically hit him pretty quickly. Ben and Ryan had left about an hour ago, after he'd guilted them into staying an hour longer than they'd intended. He'd lost track of Jace and had been roaming around the packed club that was hosting the afterparty looking for someone to get into trouble with ever since.

He saw Jace at the bar and headed that way. But as he rounded a pillar, he bumped into someone, causing his drink to slosh onto his shirt. His peripheral vision registered that he'd bumped into a woman as he pulled his now-wet shirt away from his body. "I'm so sorry," he began. "I wasn't looking..." Gabe glanced up and saw a petite brunette standing in front of him. A slow grin started to spread across her face as his eyes connected with her green ones. "Rachel?" he asked. "Holy shit, how are you?"

They both moved in for a hug instantly. "I'm good," Rachel said. "I should've known you'd be here. You and Jace always were inseparable. Where's the third Stooge?"

Gabe was gobsmacked. "He left a little while ago. He's lame," he said absently. "I can't believe you're here. Why *are* you here?"

Rachel laughed the laugh he'd always loved hearing. He hadn't seen her since they graduated college, but it felt as though no time had passed. She could have very well been standing in front of him in her cap and gown, wishing him luck in the Majors. "You know how I love my sports," she said with a wink.

And he did. They'd met when she'd asked to interview him for her sports journalism class. Well, actually, she'd asked to interview Jace, which had caused Gabe to rant for an hour about how football got all the attention. Jace had told him that if it was that big a deal to him, Gabe could go in his place.

Since Gabe couldn't back out after he'd made such a big thing out of it, he'd gone. And met Rachel. Who'd been severely disappointed to see him—a fact he'd easily overlooked because Rachel Adler was the most gorgeous creature Gabe had ever seen. He'd asked her out every day for a month after that until she finally agreed. But they'd been close to graduating, their whole lives ahead of them, and not in a place to try to make something out of it.

"So, what have you been up to? Are you a famous journalist now?" Gabe asked.

Rachel laughed. "Not so much famous. I freelance mostly. Nothing special, but I enjoy the freedom." She tucked a strand of hair behind her ear and averted her gaze from him for a second before looking back and smiling again. "And you had quite the career. Exactly like you said you would when we met."

"And you thought I was being arrogant. I told you I was going to be hot shit."

"That you did," she replied with a chuckle.

She looked around again, and Gabe could sense that she probably wasn't going to hang around. *To hell with that.* "Can I get you a drink?"

Glancing down at her glass, she sloshed the ice cubes around before draining the rest of the liquid. "Sure."

Gabe smiled and put his hand on her lower back as they walked toward the bar. Jace was still there, and Gabe put his hand on the back of Jace's neck and squeezed.

"There he is," Jace said as he pulled Gabe into an awkward one-armed hug. He was bleary-eyed and smiling like he just won . . . well, the Super Bowl.

Clapping Jace on the back, Gabe extricated himself from his friend, who looked over Gabe's shoulder where he clearly saw Rachel. His head tilted as if he was trying to figure out if he knew her or not.

"Jace, you remember Rachel, don't you? From college?"

Jace's grin grew. "Oh, yeah," he said in a way that let Gabe know his drunk-ass friend was about to embarrass him. "I remember Rachel."

Rachel smiled politely at Jace. "Good to see you again. And congratulations."

"Thanks. It's fucking crazy."

Laughing, Rachel replied, "I bet."

"Where's your keeper?" Gabe asked Jace.

"She's upstairs in VIP waiting..." Jace's eyes widened. "Oh shit. She's waiting for me. I gotta go. Nice seeing you again, Rachel."

"You too," Rachel called after him as Jace weaved haphazardly through the crowd.

"What can I get ya?" Gabe asked as he waved to the bartender.

Rachel set her glass down on the bar. "I'm going to switch to a cosmo."

"How *Sex and the City* of you."

Raising an eyebrow, Rachel replied, "How metrosexual of you."

"I love those broads." Gabe gave the bartender their order and then turned back to Rachel.

"Which one's your favorite?" she asked.

"Charlotte," he replied instantly.

"Really?"

"Of course. Small, pretty, and brunette with a great smile? What's not to like?" He smiled broadly at her, which made her roll her eyes.

"Still a flirt, I see."

"You know it. But to be honest, you're way hotter than her."

"Yeah? I love compliments. Keep 'em coming," she said as she took the drink the bartender delivered. "Thanks," she said to Gabe.

"My pleasure."

She leaned against the bar and took a sip of her drink. "So, let's get back to me being hotter than Kristin Davis."

"Is that her real name?"

"Yup. I'm surprised you even knew her name on the show."

Gabe swallowed some gin and tonic. "To be honest, Ben's girlfriend had the show on in the room while we were waiting to leave for the game, so it was fresh in my mind."

She laughed. "Well, now I'm way less impressed."

Shrugging, Gabe said, "That's okay. I'm impressive in lots of other ways."

The night progressed that way: with the two of them laughing and catching up. And more drinking. A lot more. At one point, Gabe and Rachel were in the middle of the dance floor having a retro dance-move battle. Despite Gabe doing his best Running Man, Rachel's Sprinkler was a crowd favorite. They stumbled off the floor laughing hysterically.

They ended up against a wall so they could catch their breath. Suddenly, Gabe didn't feel like laughing anymore. He watched Rachel—-the way her eyes sparkled from the strobe lights, the way the corners of her eyes crinkled, and the way she ran her fingers through her straight, chestnut-colored hair.

She locked eyes with him, and her smile faded slowly. It was replaced by a heavy-lidded seriousness Gabe hoped like hell he wasn't misreading.

He leaned toward her slowly, giving her time to back away if she wanted. But she didn't. And when their lips met, it was all Gabe could do to keep himself from pushing her against the wall and pinning her there with his body.

Rachel parted her lips, and Gabe wasted no time letting his tongue sweep into her mouth. He placed a hand on her cheek to hold her steady as he lost himself in the sensation of kissing the girl he'd always sworn he'd fallen for even though his friends said he was crazy. He hadn't known Rachel for long in college, but there had always been something about her. He was happy to discover there still was.

Eventually, he pulled away just enough to whisper against her lips. "Want to come back to my hotel?" He cringed when the words were out, sure that she'd say no. Especially since it had come out more like a proposition than he'd meant for it to.

But she surprised him by saying, "Yes," before returning her lips to his.

Gabe almost said to hell with his room, he'd have her anywhere there was space and a little bit of privacy, but he managed to maintain control of himself. He did need to be sure she was on the same page though. Which was why, before following through with it, he asked, "Are you sure? I mean, I don't want to alcohol to be the reason you're making a bad decision."

Looking like she was about to laugh, Rachel pulled back farther from him. "And sleeping with you is a bad decision?"

"Well, no. Yes. I mean, *you* might think it is. Later . . . when you've had time to—"

"Gabe?"

"Huh?"

"Take me to your hotel."

"Okay then," Gabe replied, sounding just as relieved as he was eager. And if his voice didn't convey his excitement, the fact that he was walking toward the front doors at a pace that would be considered a brisk jog for some people probably did.

★ ★ ★

Once alone in the elevator, Gabe's hands were on Rachel, sliding over her smooth skin and squeezing the meat of her ass before backing her against the mirrored wall. She moaned into his neck when he ground his erection into her. The rest of the journey back to his room was a blur as his mind was too focused on what Rachel looked like without clothes on. It wasn't even close to the first time he'd pictured that, but he'd finally get to see her for real this time.

Once they were inside, Gabe pulled off Rachel's shirt, his hands slipping up her stomach and over her thin bra. Christ, her tits were more perfect than he'd even thought possible.

"What?" Rachel pulled back with a soft laugh and looked at him in the dim light. It didn't take him long to realize why.

"I said that out loud, didn't I?"

She gave him an amused smile and nodded. "Mm-hmm."

"Sorry. I've just . . ."

"I'll forget about it if you keep doing what you were doing," she said, letting her head fall against the wall and arching her back to give Gabe better access to her chest.

Gabe loved how comfortable they were with each other already, how they could laugh during this intimate moment. It turned him on even more.

He unhooked her bra as he slid his hand down her back. Then he slipped it down her arms before tossing it behind him and hoisting her up so her legs could wrap around him.

"You have too many clothes on," she said as Gabe nipped at her neck.

"I agree. We should probably do something about that."

"We definitely should," Rachel replied.

She'd barely gotten out the words before Gabe had her moving through his hotel room toward the tall king bed and placed her on it, letting her legs dangle over the sides as he backed away to pull his Commanders jersey off. She gave him this little grin as she brought a finger to her lip and bit on its edge. He wondered if she knew how hot she was—if the act was intentional. But truthfully it didn't matter.

"Is it weird that I want to tell you how hot *your* chest is too?" she asked. The comment made Gabe smile as he popped the button of his jeans and unzipped them. He'd just begun to pull them down when Rachel said, "Leave them on." Then she sat up and grabbed his waistband to pull him toward her.

His erection, which was still straining against his jeans, perked up even further as Rachel's lips slid over his lower abs. It was an image he'd file away in his brain for future use: her head moving near his cock as his fingers tangled with her dark hair. He let out a low groan when her hand pressed against his dick. She played with it over his pants for a while before pulling down the zipper the rest of the way and yanking down his boxers enough to free him. She stroked him a few times before Gabe needed his lips back on hers.

His thumb stroked her cheek as he kissed her. Her moans grew louder as he rubbed against her, but finally he was able to pull himself away from her long enough to undo her skinny jeans and slide them down her legs. Her thong was next, and he savored the visual as the black lace traced over her skin.

He fished a condom from his wallet and tore it open. Squeezing himself as he rolled it on, he held back his orgasm. Jesus, he couldn't wait to be inside her. He hadn't thought about her in a while, but God, when he used to think about her, he'd imagine how warm and wet she was. And it was that thought that had him returning to her, guiding her down on the bed to he could press into her.

Somehow, all his fantasies couldn't even come close to the real thing. Her legs wrapped around his ass as her nails dug into his jeans to guide him even deeper inside. Then they began to move together, their bodies responding to the other's in a way that he wasn't sure he'd experienced before. She seemed to almost melt against him.

The moans and choppy breaths that escaped her had him speeding up, though he didn't exactly want this to end. He used his forearms to prop himself up so his weight wasn't on her completely as he thrust into her. Her nails were on his back, scratching over his shoulder blades before sliding under his boxers. He tensed as her fingertips brushed over his ass, and he willed himself not to come anytime soon.

He never thought he'd have Rachel Adler in his bed, and now that he did, he wanted it to be fucking memorable. And not just for him. He knew *he'd* never forget this. Though her legs were clamped around him, he pulled out almost completely and then drove back in. His thumb went to her clit the next time he withdrew, making her practically quiver beneath him. She was close, and he knew it.

A few more steady thrusts into her had Rachel begging him not to pull out again. Her words only increased the pleasure of the moment for him, and he thought about how he'd never get enough of Rachel's soft pleas. "Please, Gabe. God, yes.

Make me…" But she never finished her sentence before her body quaked with the orgasm that Gabe could feel too. Gabe continued to pound into her until her climax faded enough that he could speed up to find his own release. He wasn't even sure what he said as he came, but whatever it was, he couldn't help it. It was probably the hardest he'd come in a while, and Rachel had been the one to make him do it.

Jace wasn't the only one who'd won tonight.

CHAPTER FOUR

RACHEL

Opening her eyes, Rachel assessed her situation. She was currently in Gabe Torres's hotel room at... She didn't even know what time it was, so she stretched gingerly to reach her phone on the bedside table. *Shit. Almost ten thirty in the morning.* She hadn't meant to stay that long, or at all, but now here she was, still naked with Gabe's arm draped over her chest as he slept beside her.

Her first thought was that if Gabe's snoring hadn't woken her, she must have been really tired last night. Or drunk. Maybe mostly drunk. Her next thought was how the hell she was going to get out from under him without waking him. The only piece of clothing she could see from her current position was her bra, which made her think that the rest must be in the living room. *Why did he have to get a suite?* It would definitely make her game of Escape the Hotel Room easier if she knew where all her stuff was.

She stayed still a few more minutes before she realized that every second she spent in bed meant it was a second closer to whenever Gabe would be waking up. Wiggling slowly under the weight of his arm, she eventually freed herself and slid out of bed. Sure, it resulted in her practically falling to the floor, but she decided to look at that as a positive since she could crawl around to look for her clothes. The sound of Gabe snorting suddenly and flipping over had her freezing in place, as if the lack of movement might make her invisible.

She couldn't explain why she was so intent on leaving undetected. It was Gabe, for God's sake. She'd known him since college. Or maybe she'd known him *in* college was more accurate. They hadn't exactly kept in touch over the years, but he was still familiar. It wasn't like this was some sort of one-night stand with a stranger. No, it was more like a one-night stand with a... nonstranger, and somehow that made her feel a little better.

Then she remembered the real reason for her visit to Texas, and she felt like shit all over again. She'd been there to scour the afterparty for any sports dirt she could dig up for her job—a fact she'd kept to herself when they'd run into each other at the party.

It wasn't typically something she kept hidden from people, but she'd realized almost immediately upon running into Gabe that she didn't want him to know why she was there. He'd been so excited for Jace's win, and it seemed he hadn't lost his carefree attitude she remembered. She'd been sure that telling him she was there to look for drama wouldn't have sat well with him. She remembered from college how loyal and protective he and his friends were of each other, and she wondered if that protectiveness transferred to other athletes, or the game in general as well. For that reason, she'd only told Gabe about her freelance work and hadn't gotten into any details, and she was glad for it.

Last night had been fun. And looking at how perfectly

sculpted Gabe's body was put her at ease a little too. She definitely wouldn't call last night a mistake. It was hard to believe that the man had retired from professional baseball. He hadn't let himself go in the past five months. She took a moment to admire his chest and abs, which looked like they'd been chiseled from stone. She'd gotten to feel them last night but hadn't been able to see them well in the dark.

Somehow she was able to pull herself away from the beautiful image in front of her long enough to snatch up what she could find of her belongings. Then she slid her phone in her bag and dressed quickly before heading out the door. Once she was in the elevator, she breathed a sigh of relief. Though she didn't regret sleeping with Gabe, she also wasn't prepared to talk to him about it. She didn't want to admit that she'd lied by omission because the night would be tarnished when he found out she was an investigative reporter. Which reminded her how pissed her boss would be if he found out she came out of last night without a story. Especially after Rick's little talk.

She didn't exactly think Gabe would have any reason to *want* to talk about last night anyway. He was a professional athlete, for Christ's sake. Or he used to be. His bed was probably a merry-go-round of gorgeous women, and she was just one of many he'd taken for a ride. She knew the chance of a superstar playboy wanting to have any sort of conversation about the previous night was highly unlikely.

The fact that he was a playboy had been the main reason she hadn't agreed to go out with him in college, despite the fact that she'd been incredibly attracted to him. She hadn't wanted to date someone who, at the time, she'd been certain was only interested in her body. Plus she'd wanted to concentrate on building her career, not tarnish it by banging one of the up-

and-coming athletes she'd met at an interview. But now that she'd established her career and was confident in herself both as a reporter and as a woman, she didn't have any logical reason not to act on her desires. Yet somehow, she still found herself questioning her decision.

She couldn't even explain why she was so neurotic right now. She told herself to stop overthinking her decision. It happened, and she had to admit she'd loved it. That settled it; it definitely wasn't something she regretted.

That was, until her phone dinged with a text from a number she didn't recognize.

Forget something?

She didn't even know who it was from until a picture followed a few seconds later. And there it was: her black thong she'd been searching for this morning.

Damn it.

★ ★ ★

Even days later, thinking back on the continuation of their text conversation made her laugh.

Please throw those away. How did you get my number?

I have my ways.

You know that makes you sound like a stalker, right? And the picture of my underwear didn't help. Btw, did you throw it away? You never answered.

Then he'd sent her one of those emojis crying with laughter before writing:

You gave me your number, remember?
How drunk were you?

In the trash, don't worry.

As Rachel unplugged her phone from the charging station on her bedside table and put it in her purse before work, she almost laughed at how ridiculous the conversation had been. At least until Gabe had told her how happy he'd been to run into her and to have a safe flight back to New York. That had taken it from ridiculous to ridiculously awkward. So, in typical Rachel style, she'd written back something totally unrelated immediately in the hopes that Gabe would assume she hadn't even noticed his last text. Thankfully, he'd never questioned her about why she'd sneaked away.

The memory of her time with Gabe had her adjusting her black pencil skirt and double-checking that all the buttons on her mustard-yellow silk blouse were buttoned, almost as if the thought of sleeping with Gabriel Torres might make her clothes undress themselves. She was happy to get back to work this morning so she could take her mind off Gabe and . . . *Jesus, stop thinking about him.*

"How was Houston?" The question had come from her usually grumpy roommate, Kellan, who was sitting at their small kitchen counter sipping black coffee. When she eyed it longingly, he said, "The pot's fresh."

"Thanks," she replied, filling her favorite mug she'd gotten at Disney World a few years ago. "It was fun, I guess."

Kellan nodded as he scrolled through the news on his phone. "You get any good stories while you were down there?"

Just one I could tell some of my girlfriends about. "Nah, nothing really. Just the typical celebratory Super Bowl stuff. Why are you dressed?" she asked.

Kellan looked down at his pale-blue dress shirt and gray slacks. "Would you rather me be naked?"

Rachel rolled her eyes as she hopped up onto the barstool next to him. Kellan was as gay as he was unemployed, but he'd insisted, since they'd met years ago at a mutual friend's wedding, that Rachel had a thing for him. She didn't. She really didn't. "Please keep your clothes on," she said. "I meant why are you dressed like *that*? You have a funeral or something?"

Kellan elbowed her playfully. "What? I'm in a suit, and you think someone died?"

"Well, yeah. That, and you seem especially chipper this morning," she joked.

He laughed before replying, "I'm an asshole, but I'm not *that* big of an asshole. It doesn't make me happy when people die." She stared at him until he spoke again. "Okay, so there are certain people whose demise I might find joy in, but that's not why I'm dressed up and in a good mood. I got a job."

Rachel's eyes widened. "Really? Where? Doing what? Is it full-time? When were you going to tell me?"

"Do I get to *answer* any of the questions, or are you just gonna keep asking them?"

"Sorry," she said. "It's the reporter in me. Tell me all about it."

"I will tonight. I gotta get going though." He grabbed his suit jacket off the back of the couch and put his keys in his pocket.

"I'm meeting Lina for drinks later, but when I get back, I want to hear all about your first day on the job."

"I'm not a cop," Kellan said. "By the way, change your shirt. The yellow and black makes you look like a bumblebee."

CHAPTER FIVE

RACHEL

"You going for the queen bee look today?"

This time the comment had come from Rick, and it made Rachel laugh out loud. She'd thought about changing her shirt after Kellen had said nearly the same thing earlier but ultimately decided it didn't matter. She was only going to the office today and didn't have any interviews lined up. She'd most likely be catching up on some things she'd missed while she was traveling and probably wouldn't leave her small workspace much at all today.

All Access Sports was a magazine that covered everything and anything in the sports world. From new college players to athletes' new babies, *All Access* was interested in it. It was an odd mix that took Rachel some time to adjust to since her journalism internship had been at an extremely well-known sports news station. Ultimately, her heart was in television broadcasting, but she knew how difficult that field was to break into.

So when *All Access Sports* had offered her a position, she'd taken it. She told herself it was a stepping stone, a way to get her foot in the door, and every other cliched metaphor she could think of that would make her feel better about settling for an offer that wasn't her dream job. But the magazine had a respectable readership, and since Rachel liked most of the people she worked with—and Rick typically assigned her interesting articles, even when he was mad at her—she'd lasted longer here than she'd originally intended to.

"And you look like a lonely, middle-aged pothead," she said, finally able to think of a witty reply. It was good that things between them had gone back to normal, with them able to banter with one another.

"You say that like it's a bad thing. I'd love to be lonely. And high." Rick looked back at down at the file he'd been holding and turned a few pages. "Once the twins leave for college, I can be *all* those things." He paused for a moment and then held up the file he'd been holding. "I've got something I've been waiting to show you."

"What?" Rachel cocked her head to the side in doubt, causing Rick to grin in a way that made the wrinkles around his eyes even more pronounced. *That* got Rachel's attention. Rick only got excited about the big stories, and that immediately caused Rachel's heart rate to speed up.

He pulled his glasses down from where they'd been resting on his curly gray hair. "Maybe I'll keep you in suspense a little longer." He turned and made his way toward his office, but Rachel immediately followed.

"What is it?" She kept in stride with him, though his steps were nearly twice the length of hers.

"Interested suddenly, are we?" Rick rounded the corner to his small office. He plopped into his chair and then spun the file toward her and leaned back in his chair, his hands resting behind his head as he waited for her to peruse the documents.

Rachel sank into the chair across from him as she opened the file. She'd always had an issue reading things in a linear fashion. Even as a kid, her eagerness to finish a book had caused her eyes to jump around on the page in a way that allowed her brain to soak up all the information in pieces and somehow put it together into one cohesive whole. It was like putting together a puzzle without making the edges first. But her brain couldn't make sense of the words she saw in front of her this time. *Mike Tarino ... underground club ... drugs ...*

"Is this what I think it is?" Rachel asked, her voice barely more than a whisper, as if she were in church handling a garment worn by God himself. She didn't give Rick a chance to answer before she asked, "Where'd you get all this?" Rachel lifted the paper to see what was on the next page: a rundown of a Player's Club that catered to the best of the best in the sports world. *Fucking unicorn, my ass.* The notes were handwritten and not in Rick's script.

"Andrews got a tip from someone," Rick said with a nod toward where the intern who'd started a few weeks ago sat.

"Shit. Is Andrews his last name? I've been calling him Andrew since he started. I thought Andrew was his first name."

"His first name's Colin. Or Conner. Or something like that. Anyway, my guess is the caller didn't want to contact anyone with any sort of experience who could think of some impromptu follow-up questions to ask."

"Let me guess ... anonymous?"

Rick shook his head and gave her that sly grin again. "Nope. A former athlete."

"Who?" Rachel was nearly coming out of her seat. *This* was what she'd been waiting for.

"Cole Barnes," he replied.

Rachel felt herself deflate a little, which Rick seemed to notice because he immediately began talking. "I know, I know. The guy's a washed-up first baseman who gained a gambling debt and a bad coke habit since he retired from baseball." Rachel raised her eyebrows as if to say *My thoughts exactly*, but Rick seemed to ignore the nonverbal comment. "But that's what makes this more believable," he said, standing again because, she guessed, he was too manic now to stay in one place. "Barnes's got a chip on his shoulder because not only has he been ousted from the sports world completely, but he's claiming that Tarino kicked him out of the club."

"Tarino died months ago," Rachel said, not understanding.

"I know, but Barnes said Tarino kicked him out years ago."

"So why's he bitter about it now? Barnes is probably just looking to get back in the spotlight," she said, answering her own question. She hated having to beat back her own enthusiasm, but she couldn't let her hope outweigh her good judgment. Even though Rick seemed as excited as she was, she forced herself to remain critical of the story until it proved on the up-and-up. "Any publicity's good publicity, right?"

Rick shook his head. "I don't think that's it. Barnes said he tried to get back in when Tarino passed away and ownership of the club changed hands, but the new owner won't let him in either, so he's done with it, and this is his way of retaliating."

Rachel had to admit there was some merit to that. "Did he say who the new owner was?"

Rick shook his head. "Nope. It's the one thing he won't say. Andrews did ask him that. So I started thinking about who the new owner could be. Tarino was divorced with no kids. There isn't an obvious choice for who would've taken over the club, and we don't even know who the current members are... If this is even a real thing. The only thing we know is that Tarino lived in Philadelphia, and he had no history that we can find of extensive traveling. So it's probably a safe bet that the club's located there."

"Barnes didn't say where the club was?" she asked.

Rick shook his head. "And Andrews didn't ask. That kid's going to have to get his head out of his ass if he wants to stick around. I tried calling Barnes back personally, but he told me that he'd revealed all he had to say. If we want to find out more, we're going to have to do it without him."

Rachel felt her face scrunch up. "That's so bizarre. Why would he open this door and then try to slam it closed again?"

"Who knows. The guy's a total nutcase."

Something about it wasn't sitting right with Rachel, but she couldn't put her finger on what it was.

"I had a few people look into Tarino's finances. He had a steady stream of money coming in from somewhere, but there's no trace of where. At least not that we can find through legal means."

Rachel read a bit more of the file before looking up at Rick, who was smiling at her.

"Looks like we may have found your unicorn. How fast can you get to Philly?"

CHAPTER SIX

RACHEL

"Is that a gang member?" Kellan asked as he clutched his satchel closer to his body.

"If you're referring to the elderly man with the cane, then I'm going to go with no." Rachel rolled her eyes at Kellan's dramatics. "You grew up in the Bronx. Why are you acting like you're fresh off the prairie?"

"The homicide rate is higher in Philadelphia than New York. We're way more likely to die here."

Rachel narrowed her eyes in disbelief. "We're in Center City in the middle of the day. I think we're safe."

"That's probably what all those murdered people thought," Kellan muttered.

They continued to walk down the street in search of a market. *All Access Sports* didn't have the largest budget in the world, but Rick had secured enough money to send Rachel to Philly for the next month. Rachel initially balked at moving—even temporarily—but Rick had a valid point when he asked her how she'd be able to investigate the club if she wasn't even in the same city where it was most likely located. So she'd reluctantly capitulated and bribed Kellan into helping her move. Which she was currently regretting.

"If you don't come home, can I still keep the apartment?" Kellan asked after they'd rounded a corner.

"Will you stop talking about me dying?" Rachel looked down the street, wondering how much farther the market they'd Googled was before pulling out her phone and checking it. "Besides, we just rent there. It's not like I can leave it to you in my will."

"Do you have one of those? Because I should probably know where it is. Just in case."

Looking over at Kellan, Rachel saw a broad grin stretching his cheeks and making his dimples appear. "You're an asshole."

"I know," he said as he wrapped an arm around her shoulders. "But I'm not going to be able to hassle you on the daily for a whole month. I need to get it out of my system."

"As if that'll ever happen." She allowed herself to lean into him a little as they walked. "This neighborhood isn't bad, right?"

Kellan hesitated, and Rachel elbowed him in the ribs. Barking out a laugh, Kellan replied, "No, it's not bad. Aside from the OGs with canes, it seems perfectly safe."

Rachel smiled. Rick's assistant had found her a one-bedroom apartment that was geared toward business people and was open to short-term leases. It wasn't impressive inside by any means, but it had everything she'd need and was clean. And the buzzer on the lobby door gave her a reasonable sense of safety. It was downtown, so despite its cramped size, it was probably still costing a pretty penny, which was why Rachel couldn't waste a lot of time. She'd have to either convince Cole to talk to her or stumble upon another lead.

Having dedicated her entire life to her career, there was

no way she was going to let this story slip through her fingers. No way. Not happening. And at the end of the day, she only needed Barnes to point her in the right direction. He would be the first in what would undoubtedly be an extremely long trail of bread crumbs.

"You should feed me," Kellan said abruptly, pulling Rachel out of her thoughts.

"I thought that's why we were going to the market."

Kellan's face scrunched up. "That'll take too long. You should buy me dinner. And dessert. And drinks."

Rachel sighed heavily, but it was more for show than anything else. "Where would His Highness like to go?"

Eyes growing wide, Kellan looked around excitedly. "There," he said as he pointed to a small bistro across the street.

"Looks expensive," Rachel said dryly.

"I know. It's perfect."

They waited for the light to change before crossing the street. "So where are you gonna start?" Kellan asked.

Rachel had blabbed the entire story over a bottle of wine after Rick had offered her the project. She'd been brimming with excitement, and since Kellan was unable to escape since he lived with her, he'd been subjected to her gushing.

"Ugh, I don't know," Rachel said. "I've been racking my brain for how to begin, but I've got nothing."

They entered the small restaurant and were told there would be a bit of a wait unless they wanted to eat at the bar. Kellan craned his neck toward the bar before nodding to Rachel. "The bar will work," she said.

The deep mahogany bar had matching stools surrounding it. They were almost all available, so Kellan and Rachel chose two off to one end and settled in. The bartender grabbed their orders quickly—a whiskey sour for Kellan and a 7&7 for Rachel—and handed them menus.

"What looks good to you?" Rachel asked.

"Everything," Kellan replied.

Rachel chuckled. "I think I'm going to get the tomato-and-mozzarella salad."

Kellan shot her a disgusted face. "Who gets a salad with a menu like this?"

"I do."

Sighing, Kellan said, "Guess I'll just have to order enough carbs for both of us."

The bartender returned with their drinks and took their orders. Kellan lived up to his promise, ordering the bistro's "famous" lasagna and a side of penne. He even threw in a flirty wink for good measure—which the bartender did not return.

"You have no shame," Rachel said to Kellan when the bartender walked away.

"Never know unless you try," Kellan replied before taking a sip of his drink.

Rachel picked up hers and put the straw in her mouth, but just as liquid hit her tongue, a voice startled her from behind.

"No cosmos? Charlotte would be so disappointed."

Choking, Rachel grabbed a napkin and covered her mouth. When she'd gotten herself under control, she turned. *Fuck my life.* "Hi, Gabe."

GABE

"Of all the bistros in all the world," Gabe said. He couldn't believe what he was seeing. When he'd been walking back from the restroom and seen Rachel sitting at the bar, Gabe had done a double take. *What the hell is she doing here?* "What the hell are you doing here?" he asked with a smile.

"I'm, uh, here for work," she replied. She seemed thrown, which shouldn't really surprise Gabe. He felt thrown too. Her eyes darted to the guy next to her, and Gabe noticed him for the first time. He'd been so focused on Rachel he hadn't even processed that anyone was with her. Extending his hand, Gabe said, "Gabe Torres."

"Kellan Hughes."

"Nice to meet you," Gabe said. It was weird as fuck talking to the guy, and Gabe couldn't decide why. He was normally social to a fault, but something about the dude with Rachel rubbed him the wrong way.

"You too." Kellan looked quickly over at Rachel before bringing his eyes back to Gabe and flashing him the largest, fakest smile Gabe had seen in quite some time. Gabe immediately returned it because he couldn't resist making the moment more awkward.

Turning to Rachel, Gabe said, "So, here for work, huh? You want to interview me again like you did back in the day?" He laughed, but Rachel seemed to blanch a little, though she recovered quickly.

She cleared her throat before speaking. "I don't know that I'm up for interviewing the great Gabriel Torres." Her lips twitched at the corners as she tried to fight a smile.

It made Gabe relax a little. "Hey, I'm here with someone. You mind if we come sit with you guys?" Gabe asked as he gestured to the open seats next to Rachel.

Gabe almost cursed his impulsiveness, but the reality

was that he wanted to hang out with Rachel more, even if he was crashing a date or whatever was going on. At least he had Camille with him, so he wouldn't be a total third wheel.

Both of the people in front of him stumbled over their words for a second before Rachel smiled and told him he should absolutely join them.

"Great," Gabe replied. "I'll be right back." This was a bad idea. That guy was probably Rachel's boyfriend. For all Gabe knew, she was dating him when she fucked Gabe senseless after the Super Bowl. It would explain why Rachel seemed so uncomfortable, but he couldn't take it back now.

He rushed over to a high-top table by the window where Camille was sitting. "Hey. I need you to finally accept your true feelings for me and show that couple sitting at the bar how much you love me. Okay? Great. Come on." Gabe made a grab for her drink, but Camille pulled it out of his reach.

"First of all, *you're* the only one who needs to accept my true feelings for you. Second, no. Third, they're not a couple."

"What part were you saying 'no' to?"

"The part where I pretend to love you in front of strangers."

Gabe's shoulders fell. "But that's what I need you for the most."

"Why?"

"Because that's Rachel." Gabe had told Camille all about his sexcapades in Texas. He had left out how disappointed he'd been when he'd woken up to find Rachel gone, but he was pretty sure Camille knew anyway. It was scary how well she'd come to know him in such a short time.

"I'm not making a girl jealous. It's against girl code."

"But we're working off bro code right now," Gabe argued.

"There's just one problem with that. I'm not your bro, bro."

"We'll let them assume."

Camille looked at him as if he were crazy. "Why do we need to do that?"

"Because she's on a date, so I want to be on one too."

"God, you're such a teenager. And she's definitely *not* on a date."

Gabe looked quickly over his shoulder. Rachel and Kellan were whispering. They looked tense, and Gabe wondered if Kellan suspected something. "How do you know?" he asked when he returned his attention to Camille.

"Because that guy is not batting for your team."

Gabe stood there quietly for a second before saying, "I know that's a baseball analogy for my benefit, but I don't know what the hell it means."

Camille sighed as though dealing with Gabe was the most trying thing she'd ever done in her life. "He's gay."

Gabe's head whipped around to look at Kellan again before he could think about what he was doing. "What? How do you know?"

Camille gave him a look that let Gabe know how stupid she thought he was.

"Stop. You're a lesbian. I'm not trusting your gaydar when it comes to dudes."

"He has a murse."

"What the fuck is a 'murse'?" Gabe asked.

"A man purse."

Gabe sneaked a peek at the large bag that was hanging from the back of Kellan's chair. "So? I see guys with those all the time. You of all people should know better than to stereotype," Gabe scolded.

"The strap is rainbow colored."

"Maybe he likes bright colors."

"Gabriel," Camille said in a tone that let Gabe know she'd had enough of his silliness. "You're being obtuse, and it's not cute. She is not dating that guy. So we can absolutely go over there, but we're not lying about our relationship. Got it?"

Gabe took a deep breath. He always bordered on hyper, and he'd let it get away from him for a second. Calmer, he said, "Yeah. I got it."

Camille gave him a small smile. "Good. Now let's go talk to your girl."

"She's not my girl," Gabe retorted, reaching for Camille's drink again so he could carry it for her.

Looking over at Rachel and then back at Gabe, Camille said, "No, but you want her to be."

It wasn't a question, but Gabe wanted to respond anyway. "My feelings for her are almost ten years old. I hardly know who she is now."

Camille smiled at him. "Well, let's go find out, shall we?"

CHAPTER SEVEN

GABE

With classic Gabe bravado that was more for show than anything else, Gabe led Camille to where Rachel was sitting. He'd mastered the art of exuding confidence when he didn't really feel it when he was a teenager trying to get scouted. No one wanted to waste time on a skinny kid with a self-esteem issues—a kid who nearly gave himself an ulcer worrying about how he was going to hack it in major league baseball... If he even made it there. That was why his mom had been so adamant that he go to college first—which only led to more worry since he still wasn't great at reading English at the time, despite having been in the US since he was twelve.

But she'd been right. Gabe hadn't been ready to be on his own in the world and make more money than he would've known what to do with. He'd needed to grow up more. Get a foundation under him. It had been a gamble, but it had paid off tenfold. Gabe had no doubt that most of his professional success came as a result of his having played collegiate ball, and not because of the skills he'd honed. In school, he'd learned how to *actually* believe in himself, rather than faking it. And that self-assurance had bled into every aspect of his life—

except, of course, his interactions with Rachel Adler.

Rachel's straight white teeth were gleaming as she smiled at them. Her long brown hair fell over her shoulders and was so shiny it reflected the lights. "Rachel, this is my friend Camille. Camille, Rachel. And this is Kellan," he tacked on so as not to be blatantly rude. He'd never hoped so much that a guy was gay. Well, there was that one time he'd thought Ben was coming out to him, but that was a misunderstanding. He hoped this wasn't. The thought of Rachel dating someone else did things to him he didn't want to focus on.

Everyone exchanged greetings, and Camille and Gabe sat down next to them. There was an awkward silence for a minute, and Gabe racked his brain to try to figure out how to fill.

Rachel turned to Camille, who was beside her. "So, Camille, how do you know Gabe?" Her voice sounded off, like she was trying too hard to make it come off as an innocent question.

Gabe knew it was wishful thinking that she'd been bitten by the same jealousy bug that nipped him.

"We met through a mutual friend," Camille explained. "How about you?"

Gabe would've kissed Camille if it wouldn't have gotten him punched. He'd already told her all about how he knew Rachel, but Camille was acting like she'd never heard of her. The last thing Gabe needed was for Rachel to think he was obsessed with her or something. Camille was his bro after all.

"We went to college together. I accidentally interviewed him once," Rachel said with a sly grin in his direction.

"Please. We both know you asking Jace was all just an elaborate ploy to get close to me," Gabe said.

Rachel looked at Camille and rolled her eyes. "Oh darn, he's figured me out," she said dryly.

"What do you do, Kellan?" Gabe asked.

"I just got a job as a copywriter for a marketing firm in New York."

Gabe smiled. "I have absolutely no idea what that is, but congrats."

Kellan laughed. "They're a start-up. I'm not too sure they know what a copywriter is either."

"You like it so far?" Camille asked.

Kellan shrugged. "It's okay. It's a job, so I can't complain. I was about a week away from selling my ass for cash, so it's a step in the right direction."

The girls chuckled, but before he could think better of it, Gabe said, "We know someone who did that! Don't we, Camille?"

As Camille slowly panned toward him, Gabe realized he maybe shouldn't have blurted that out. "I mean, she pretended she did that. Or lied about it." Camille's raised eyebrows let him know he wasn't making things better.

"That sounds like quite a story," Rachel said.

"Yes, but it's one we're not going to tell, is it, Gabriel?" Camille's voice was friendly—probably for Rachel and Kellan's benefit because her eyes were like lasers trying to flay the skin off Gabe.

He made motion over his mouth like he was closing a zipper, which made Camille look exasperated with him.

"Well, I'm glad it didn't come to that," Kellan said, effectively redirecting the conversation. "My roommate is a real hard-ass, so if I hadn't found something soon, she was going to throw me out." He gave Rachel a smug look, which made her slap him on the arm.

"No, she wasn't."

"Wait, you guys are roommates?" Gabe asked, a little louder than he'd intended.

"Yeah. We met at a wedding a few years ago, and she's been obsessed with me since, even though I keep trying to tell her I'm not into her . . . type," Kellan explained.

"Yeah, that's not even remotely the case," Rachel said.

"Please. You asked me to move in with you after we'd known each other for three days."

"Because you told me you were going to have to become a rent boy if you couldn't find an affordable place to live."

"Stop acting like you saving me from a life of prostitution was a selfless act. You just didn't want to share me with the rest of Manhattan."

"Oh my God," Camille interjected. She turned to Gabe. "They're just like us."

"Like looking in a mirror," Gabe replied, his tone serious. "Except . . . who's the almost–rent boy in our situation?"

"Definitely me," Camille said.

"That makes sense," Gabe said with a nod.

Camille did that slow panning thing again. "And why exactly does that make sense to you?"

Gabe tilted his head a little. "Why did it make sense to you?"

"Because I'm the poor, gay one."

"That's why it makes sense to me too."

"Mm-hmm," Camille said before turning back to Rachel. "So what brings you to Philly?"

Gabe's ears perked up at the question. Rachel hadn't given him much of an answer when he'd asked before.

"For work," Rachel said before picking up her drink and taking what seemed to be a gulp. "I'm a journalist. So I'm here on an assignment," she finished.

"That's neat. What's the story?"

Rachel's mouth opened and closed a couple times. Gabe felt like he was watching a fish that had been yanked out of the water.

The silence stretched on until Kellan interjected, "She's writing about what goes on in men's locker rooms."

She's . . . what? That seemed like a strange idea for a sports article. Despite the press being a common presence in the locker room after games, most of the time it was a safe space for the athletes. It was odd for a team to willingly crack open the doors and let a reporter have free rein in there.

"That's not it, exactly," Rachel corrected. She turned her head to look at Kellan, but Gabe couldn't tell what that look consisted of. Judging by the way Kellan shrugged—an *I was only trying to help* kind of gesture—Gabe guessed it wasn't pleasant.

"I'm doing an article on the behind-the-scenes stuff athletes endure, but I won't actually be going into the locker rooms. It will mostly focus on the stresses athletes face off the court or field, or . . . whatever."

"Oh. That sounds interesting," Gabe said. "Are you mostly focusing on hockey? Since that's the only sport in season right now? Basketball doesn't count because it's boring."

"Um, well, uh, no, no, I'm focusing on all sports. The players don't have to be in season to be able to tell me about their experiences." Rachel took another drink. "And I'm not limited to athletes here. Philly was just more central to travel out of since it's close to Baltimore and Washington and New

Jersey, and … other places."

"That makes sense," Gabe said.

"Good," Rachel sighed. Her eyes widened. "I mean it's good because a strong story should always make sense. Like the concept. If the concept doesn't make sense, then the article probably won't, either."

Gabe smiled. "I can see how it would work like that."

Rachel gave a soft laugh, which seemed to relax her whole body. Gabe wasn't sure what caused her to get so tense when she was talking about her article. Maybe she was nervous about talking to the players or something. Which was a problem Gabe could fix.

"I could introduce you to some guys who'd be happy to talk to you. You probably have guys who've already agreed, but if you need more, I can definitely make some calls."

Rachel's eyes brightened at his offer. "That'd be great. I'll let you know."

The conversation flowed more easily after that. Eventually, Camille moved to sit on the other side of Kellan, and Gabe slid closer to Rachel.

"You should let me take you to dinner while you're here. When you have time, of course." Gabe tried to not get his hopes up that she'd agree. This was a girl who'd sneaked out of his hotel room at butt-fuck o'clock to get away from him. But seeing her here made it feel like fate had intervened, and he'd be damned if he didn't at least try to shore up plans to see her again.

She smiled softly at him. "I'd like that."

"Really?" He should've tried to hide how surprised he was at her easy acquiescence, but screw it. Her answering grin told him she'd liked it anyway.

"Yes, really."

"You around Wednesday?" Business at the club had slowed down a little since the Super Bowl. It seemed everyone hibernated until March Madness kicked off and hockey playoffs began. Mike's business logs had reported an annual decline in member attendance during this time of year, so at least Gabe knew not to blame himself. And it also meant he could easily sneak away for a date midweek.

"I can be," Rachel replied.

Gabe might have imagined the sultry look in her eyes, but he sure hoped he hadn't.

RACHEL

Rachel slapped Kellan's arm again as they walked down the busy city street. It was dark, and Rachel was surprised by how much time had passed inside the bar. It had felt like an hour, but had clearly been closer to three. "Locker rooms? Really?"

Kellan rubbed his arm where she'd hit him. "What? I was only trying to help. You were just sitting there like a jackass."

"Telling Gabe that I'm writing a story about guys in locker rooms was you helping? I'd hate to see what you'd say if you were trying to sabotage me."

"It's the first thing that came to mind. It's not my fault that my knowledge of sports is limited to fantasizing about them having orgies after games."

Staring at him, Rachel said, "Stop acting like a stereotype."

"What stereotype would that be?"

"That all men have sex on the brain twenty-four seven."

Kellan laughed. "Sweetie, that is *not* a stereotype. Even

your precious Gabe probably thought about it at least twenty times while we were there."

Rachel scoffed. "He did not." She was already regretting telling Kellan about her one-night stand.

"Such a mature response," Kellan teased. "And yes, he was. It was written all over his face when he looked at you. That boy is smitten."

"Did you just say 'smitten'?"

Kellan flipped her off and continued. "Why do you think he asked you on a date? Because he wanted to spend more time with your sparkling personality?"

"I don't know why I hang out with you."

Kellan sighed dramatically. "We've been over why."

"You're the worst."

Kellan slung an arm around Rachel's shoulders. "I know. It's part of my charm."

"If you say so," Rachel muttered, but she let herself lean into him a little.

"You need to be careful with him, ya know," Kellan said softly after a few steps.

Letting her head rest against his chest as they walked awkwardly down the street, Rachel replied, "I know." And she did know. Gabe's reasons for asking her out were romantic in nature. Or at the very least sexual—which was a concern she didn't care to focus on at the moment. If she wasn't careful to keep some distance, she'd end up leading him on when she knew it was a bad idea to mix business with pleasure.

But part of her also knew that she'd said yes to the date because she—Rachel the person, not Rachel the reporter—wanted to go out with Gabe. She liked being around him—*really* liked being around him, if she let her mind drift to their encounter after the Super Bowl. Enjoyed his energy and humor and genuineness.

Kellan gave her a squeeze. "Be careful with yourself too."

Rachel replied with the only truth she had. "I'll try."

CHAPTER EIGHT

RACHEL

"That's really what you like best about Philadelphia?" Rachel asked, staring at the bronze statue.

"Yeah. Why's that weird? Rocky Balboa's a local hero."

"He's not a *real* hero. He's from a movie. And he didn't do anything that was heroic. He was just a boxer." Rachel recognized her mistake so quickly she should have been able to prevent herself from even making it.

But before she could take back her words or twist their meaning into something less insulting, Gabe was already talking. "Just a boxer? *Just* a boxer," he repeated, making her feel even worse when he emphasized the word. "The next thing you'll tell me is that Abraham Lincoln was just a president, and Jesus was just a carpenter."

"Did you really compare Rocky to Lincoln and Jesus?"

Gabe stared at her. "That depends. Did you really insult your own people?"

"Presidents? Or biblical figures?" What the hell was Gabe talking about?

"No, not presidents," Gabe clarified. "Athletes. You're a sports reporter, aren't you? Shouldn't you try to stay on their good side?" Despite his demonstrative gestures and defensiveness, she could tell Gabe was only giving her a hard time.

"I wouldn't really call that 'insulting.' Heroes are cops and firefighters. And military or someone who saves a dog who gets stuck in a tree or something." She saw Gabe's smile begin to form, and she could tell he was holding back a laugh. "What?"

"Do a lot of dogs get stuck in trees?" His arms were crossed over his chest, and he was looking at her with an arrogance only Gabriel Torres could make charming.

"Shut up," she said, stepping toward him so she could give him a playful punch to the arm. "Cats. And you know what I mean. Rocky's a fictional boxer."

"We may have to agree to disagree," Gabe said.

Shaking her head, Rachel let her laugh be her reply before grabbing Gabe's hand to pull him in front of the statue. "Take a selfie with me and Rocky," she said, already pulling out her phone and angling it up so the shot could have all three of them in it.

"I don't think Mr. Balboa gave his consent to be photographed," Gabe said.

"You didn't give yours either, but I'm still taking the picture," Rachel said. "Now say cheese."

"You're very bossy," Gabe replied as she snapped a few pictures.

Rachel shrugged as she flipped through the pictures to find the best one. Then she sent it to Gabe. "I texted it to you."

"Oh, cool. Thanks. You care if I tweet it?"

"No, go ahead."

"You have an Instagram account? I'll tag you."

The answer to Gabe's question was yes, but she realized

quickly that she shouldn't disclose that. Her profile said she worked at *All Access,* a fact she'd neglected to share with Gabe when they'd run into each other after the Super Bowl, and that she felt awkward about announcing now. Also, the fact that Gabe was a former athlete in Philly, where she was tasked with finding out about a club for athletes, made her less inclined to share the tidbit with him. She knew it was inevitable, but the longer she could keep it to herself, the better. She finally went with "My account's private," which she felt less guilty about saying since it was the truth.

Once Gabe shared the picture of them, the two headed to a restaurant that Gabe had suggested on Boathouse Row. She was glad he'd planned the outing without asking for her input because she'd only been to Philly a handful of times and didn't have any suggestions about where to go. He'd taken her to the art museum first. Not striking her as the artistic type, she'd initially been shocked that he'd chosen to take her there. But when she'd asked him about his interest in art, he'd said he'd never really understood it, but that since Rachel's mother was a painter, he thought maybe Rachel could explain some things to him.

The gesture had been sweet because not only had she been surprised that Gabe remembered the detail about her mother—a fact Rachel hadn't even remembered mentioning— he'd also made her feel a little more comfortable in a strange city by giving her the opportunity to show *him* around too.

"So, what else have you been up to since we left college?" Gabe asked her once they'd sat down.

Since he already knew she was a journalist—though not the full extent of it—she wasn't sure what he was asking exactly. "Nothing much. Just the usual. Did an eight-year stint in the slammer but got released for good behavior."

"No one calls it 'the slammer' anymore," Gabe said, his expression unaffected by her joke.

"I just did." Then she gave him a cheesy grin, which caused him to laugh. His teeth appeared almost whiter than the crisp Henley he had on, and now that she was studying it, she couldn't pull her attention away from the way the material stretched over his chest. She remembered how it felt against her palms as she'd run her hands over him. She could almost feel the soft hairs tickling her skin at the thought.

Gabe put his elbows on the table and folded his hands slightly below his chin—a movement that made his biceps look like they might cause the cuffs around them to rip as they stretched. She was lost in the deep brown of his eyes and in the way his bronze skin looked even darker against the white of his shirt when Gabe's voice startled her out of her visual foreplay. "You all right?" he asked.

"Yeah. Yes. I'm fine. Just thinking." And, so Gabe didn't have time to ask her about what, she told him about what she'd really been up to after college. She'd gotten an internship at a major sports news station, but the opportunity hadn't resulted in a career at one. So since then she'd been taking some freelance work as it came and writing for a smaller publication. "Other than that, I've just been living the small-town girl, big-city life in New York."

"You like it there?"

"I do. It's expensive as hell though." She quickly realized that Gabe probably wouldn't be able to relate: He'd been paid millions of dollars from the time he'd started his career. Paying seven dollars for a coffee was certainly no big deal to him. "And I don't get to go home much. It's tough to find time to fly all the way to Oregon. Weekend trips aren't really worth it."

"Yeah, I definitely get that. My mom still refuses to leave Puerto Rico." The way Gabe stirred his iced tea with his straw gave her the impression that the distance bothered him more than he let on.

"I didn't even realize that's where she lived." The admission made her feel guilty because she realized that she knew less about Gabe's life than he knew about hers. "Were you born there?"

"Yeah. My aunt and uncle moved to the US years ago with my cousins, and a little while after they left, my mom sent me to live with them. She thought I'd get a better education here."

Rachel tried to imagine what it would be like to move to a different country as a kid, but as hard as she tried, she couldn't. Her childhood had always been easy: two parents, two older brothers who gave her a hard time but were as protective as they were annoying. It wasn't until her father passed away when she was in college that she really had to deal with any serious struggle. "How old were you when you moved here?" she asked him.

"Twelve. But I'd still go home every summer as long as my aunt and uncle had the money to send me. There was no way my mom could've afforded it, but my uncle made a pretty good living. And once I was old enough to get a job, I saved the money myself."

Rachel wanted to ask about Gabe's father, but since he hadn't mentioned the man, she figured he didn't want to talk about him. "She's never wanted to move here so she could be closer to you?"

Gabe pulled off a piece of bread and popped it into his mouth as he shook his head. "Nope. She's lived there all her life, and her English isn't great. When my grandparents passed, they left my mom the house that she grew up in. She loves that place. Won't even let me buy her a nice beach house or anything."

"That's kind of sweet," Rachel said, thinking about how so many people would probably take advantage of an offer like that. "Do you go there much?"

"Whenever I can. I couldn't get there at all during the season when I played though. Now that I'm retired, visiting should be easier."

It made Rachel wonder why he wasn't there now. "Have you been back a lot since you retired?" She found herself genuinely wanting to know more about Gabe, which was a change for her. Having been single for a while and having a job that required her to interview people while maintaining a professional distance meant that it was rare that she cared on a personal level.

"Not as much as I'd like to. Twice, I think. For like two weeks at a time."

"Oh, wow," she replied. "I'm surprised you didn't want to stay longer."

"I did. But it's hard to leave for long periods of time. I'm used to living out of a suitcase, but I'm kind of sick of it, to be honest."

The two leaned back to let the server put down their meals. She asked if Gabe and Rachel wanted anything else, but they said they were fine.

"So what are you doing with all your new free time?"

Gabe cleared his throat, looking slightly uncomfortable at the question. "Stuff," he said, shrugging.

"What are you interested in? Do you have any hobbies

or anything you've picked up?" She sounded like a nosy preschooler, and she knew it. But some habits died hard. And asking questions was one of them.

"Some, yeah."

"Like what?" Rachel hadn't even taken a bite of her chicken yet, and she realized that to avoid seeming like some sort of military interrogator, she should probably do her best to act casual.

Gabe's muscles seemed to tense a bit with the question, as if he hadn't been anticipating it. Though she couldn't imagine why. It seemed like the next logical one to ask. Which was why she didn't hesitate to ask it.

"Just some volunteer work," Gabe said. "Jace has been working with a local organization for years that helps sick kids. It lifts their spirits when they can meet some of their favorite athletes. It's how Jace met his fiancée, Aly, actually. She's a pediatric oncologist."

"That's so sweet," Rachel said. "I bet the kids love seeing all of you." She paused for a moment, taking a sip of her iced tea and doing her best to act casual as she asked, "That doesn't take up that much of your time, does it?"

Gabe shifted in his seat before answering. "No, I guess not. A few hours a week. But I've got some other things in the works."

Rachel waited for him to continue, but he didn't. "You weren't always this hesitant to talk about yourself," she teased.

Gabe laughed. "I've always wanted to help animals. I've donated money to the Humane Society and places like that in the past, but I'd really like to get hands-on and make a difference." She noticed Gabe eating faster, stabbing his pasta with his fork and popping it into his mouth between sentences.

"I love animals, too. Living in New York was the first time I didn't have a pet in the house. I miss having someone to cuddle with."

"You know I've been told I have puppy-dog eyes?" Gabe said, waggling his eyebrows at her.

"You're ridiculous," she said, though she couldn't deny it was cute. *He* was cute. "What are you planning to do with animals?"

"Um . . . You know, normal stuff. Like find homes for strays and rescues. Things like that." Gabe nodded as if he were the one listening to the information and not the one delivering it.

"Are you doing volunteer work for a certain rescue organization or . . ." Rachel's question trailed off as she waited for Gabe to fill in the rest.

He finished chewing and took a sip of his drink before he spoke. "Yeah. Well, I mean I *will* be. Right now I've just been doing what I can at home."

"What do you mean 'at home'?"

Rachel had no idea what he meant by that, and from the look on Gabe's face, he seemed just as confused as she was. "Uh . . . I've taken in a few animals, given them some food and a place to sleep. And some love," he tacked on almost as an afterthought. "Then I try to find them a good home or a shelter that doesn't euthanize them."

"Wow, that's impressive. So you visit sick kids and you're saving the lives of animals one kitten at a time."

Letting out an audible breath, Gabe nodded slowly. "I'm guess I'm pretty unbelievable, aren't I?"

It was as if Gabe had taken the words right from her brain before she had a chance to utter them. Sexy *and* selfless was a combination that was hard to come by. "That's exactly what I was thinking," she said with a smile.

GABE

Jace nearly spit out his beer on the pool table at Gabe's words, but he was able to cover his mouth in time to prevent the mess.

"Watch it," Gabe said, "I'm not replacing the felt on this thing because your saliva's all over it."

"Sorry," Jace said once he was able to swallow what was in his mouth. "I just learned you told Rachel that you've been adopting feral cats so they aren't put down. It would've been your fault if the table got ruined."

Gabe glared at him before lining up for his next shot. "I did *not* say anything to her about feral cats. She just assumed that, so I ran with it."

"Oh. Okay," Jace said dryly. "That's much better."

"Shut up." Gabe plopped himself down on the leather stool at the high-top table nearby and tossed his pool stick back and forth between his hands. "What would *you* have said?

"Not that."

"This woman's gonna think I'm a loser if I tell her I've been sitting around on my ass for the past however many months because I'm too lazy to do anything. And I can't exactly tell her I've been spending my time at the secret club I've been running."

"Well, that I agree with," Jace said. "But I still feel like the nonprofit animal shelter out of your house route wasn't your best option."

"I'm not good at thinking on my feet."

"You don't say?"

"So maybe I could've come up with something else—"

"*Anything* else."

Gabe stared at his best friend but didn't acknowledge his comment. "But that's what I thought of, so now that's what I'm stuck with."

Jace laughed. "Just when I start to think you can't be any more of a dumbass, you exceed my expectations."

"Thank you," Gabe said, a good-natured smile spreading across his face. "I'm glad my antics are at least entertaining to someone."

"I'm sure they were entertaining to Rachel too. There's no way she believed you opened a pet motel in your living room."

Gabe took another sip of his beer as he tried not to act like Jace's comment worried him. If Rachel thought he was lying last night, that didn't bode well for any future relationship with her. "First of all, I'm not running a pet motel."

"I know you're not."

Gabe rolled his eyes. "And second of all, if I did have stray animals in my house, they wouldn't be in my living room when I have two extra bedrooms. And it would be a *ho*tel, not a *mo*tel. My place is nice."

"Maybe you should start one," Jace said. "You seem like you've given it a lot of thought."

"Just take your turn before I beat you with your cue."

"Okay, okay, I'm shooting." Jace held up his hands before lining up his shot. "By the way, what's going on with that dick, Barnes? He still giving you a hard time?"

"Nah, haven't heard much from him lately. Hopefully it'll stay that way."

"That's good. Maybe he's given up."

"I hope so. Running this place is tough enough without worrying about bitter ex-addicts trying to threaten their way back in. One of the bartenders quit suddenly the other day. She said one of the guys put his hands on her, but she wouldn't even tell me who. Now I have to worry about the douchebag doing it again, and I have to find a replacement for her."

"Shit," Jace said, looking sympathetic.

"I know. It's not like I can place an ad on fucking Craigslist or something. Where the hell do I look for a bartender for a club that's not supposed to exist?"

"I have no idea, man. Did Mike leave any tips or instructions or anything about that stuff?"

"Not about that. He left info about the vendors and what paperwork people need to sign and stuff. But that's really it. You'd be surprised how many little things pop up that I have no idea how to handle." Exasperated, Gabe ran a hand through his hair. "Lately I've been thinking I shouldn't have even agreed to this. I'm not cut out for it."

Jace came over to him and put an arm around Gabe's shoulders, squeezing him so hard against his own body it almost hurt. "Nah, you'll figure it out. You always do." Gabe was just about to thank him for the kind words when Jace added, "And if you don't, the pet motel thing sounds like a solid Plan B."

Gabe glared at him. "I told you it was a *ho*tel. And I hate you."

"No, you don't," Jace replied.

And they both knew Jace was right: Gabe could never hate his friend. Not when he loved him so damn much.

CHAPTER NINE

RACHEL

Rachel poured herself another cup of caramel coffee and threw in a splash of cream. It was almost ten in the morning, and she'd been thinking about the story she was supposed to be investigating since she'd woken up over two hours ago. Rick would want her—no, *expect* her—to have some sort of credible information or a lead of some kind if he were going to keep her in Philadelphia. And at this point, she hadn't even begun to look into anyone who might help her find out about the club.

Now it wasn't just that the story was important to her; she liked spending time with Gabe. He was funny, and sweet, and generous. And she wanted no part of going back to New York when she could be here hanging out with him. Or kissing him. Yes, she decided she'd definitely like to kiss him again.

But she couldn't shake the fact that having any sort of a romantic relationship with Gabe was, ethically speaking, a poor idea. She'd told him that she was here as her first stop on a profile of professional athletes, which was a lie in itself. And the more she thought about it, the guiltier she felt.

But there was no way she could tell him about her real subject of her story. She needed to find a reason to be in Philly that she could share with Gabe. Her mind had gone in circles trying to come up with the perfect solution, but in a few hours, she'd come up with absolutely nothing. Plus, if she didn't find a solid lead soon, she knew that soon enough Rick would tell her to call it quits and head back to New York with or without the information she'd come here for. *All Access* certainly didn't have unlimited funds. But it wasn't Rachel's style to give up so easily. Something would come to her eventually. She was sure of it.

And as she turned on the TV with the hopes of giving herself a break from thoughts of Gabe and the article, that something was staring her right in the face.

GABE

When Gabe saw Rachel's name come up on his phone, he rose from the couch immediately and headed toward his kitchen to answer. "Hey," he said, doing his best not to sound as thrilled as he felt that she was calling him. They'd gone out the previous night, and if he expected to hear from her, it wasn't this soon.

"Hey," she replied. "What's going on?"

Gabe glanced over his island at the guys who were lounging on his dark brown leather couches. "Nothing really. I'm hanging out with Jace and another guy who used to play for the Premiers."

There was silence on the other end of the line before Rachel spoke again. "Oh, well, I was calling to see if you wanted to grab a bite to eat or a drink or something. I had an idea I wanted to run by you, but don't want to interrupt—"

"No, you're not interrupting anything. We're just watching college basketball."

"Oh, okay." Her voice sounded lighter, and he thought he recognized excitement in it. "Well, would it be weird for me to come over and hang with all of you for a little while? It'll be like I'm one of the guys, I swear."

Gabe laughed, thinking that he would never be able to think of Rachel as another dude, even if she did have a passion for sports. "It's only weird because you asked if it would be weird."

"Oh, um . . ."

"I'm kidding," said Gabe. "Come on over."

"Great! I'll see you in a little while."

"Rachel?"

"Yeah?"

"Don't you need my address?"

"Yes, yes." She laughed softly, and he could tell he'd gotten her a little flustered. "I need your address. That'd probably be a good idea."

"I'll text it to you as soon as I hang up," he assured her. "I'm glad you're coming."

He hadn't given much thought to his last statement before he'd said it, but he was happy he'd told her. And when she responded with a "Me too," Gabe smiled more brightly than he had in a long time.

Gabe must've still been smiling when he came back to the family room because Manny raised an eyebrow at him before asking, "Why do you look like that?"

"Like what?" Gabe asked, doing his best to play it cool.

"That was probably his girl," Jace said before Manny could describe the goofy grin that Gabe was sure Manny had been referring to.

"She's not *my* girl," Gabe said, thinking about how Camille had referred to Rachel the same way. He wished it were true. Picking up his beer bottle from the table, he settled back into his favorite chair.

"So you're hanging out with someone else's girl?" Manny asked, his eyes widening. "You better hope whoever he is doesn't find out."

Gabe rolled his eyes. "She's not anyone else's girl either. I mean, I thought she was with this one guy, but then Camille told me he wasn't on our team, and—"

"He's a ballplayer too? What team does he play for?" Manny asked.

"The gay one," Gabe answered, feeling vindicated that he wasn't the only one who was confused by the reference. He'd have to tell Camille about it later.

"Oh, gotcha." Manny slapped his thigh and fell back in laughter. Manny had always been a bigger guy, and since he'd gained more than a few pounds after his retirement three years ago, his stomach bounced with every chuckle. When he finally calmed down, he asked, "So you gonna hit that, or what, man?"

Gabe rolled his eyes, causing Manny to say that he guessed Gabe already had.

"A gentleman never kisses and tells," Gabe said.

Manny stared blankly before looking around and declaring that he didn't see any gentlemen there.

Gabe punched his friend hard in the shoulder. "She's coming over soon, so you better not ruin this for me."

"We won't," Manny promised him. "You'll probably ruin it for yourself before we get the chance."

CHAPTER TEN

GABE

The second he'd realized his place was a mess, Gabe had scrambled to straighten it up. He didn't want Rachel to think he was a slob, so he'd grabbed all the empty beer bottles and tossed them in the recycling, quickly put the dirty dishes in the dishwasher—even the ones he'd have to take back out to wash by hand—and rearranged the snacks he had out. Then he grabbed some plates and napkins and set them down.

Jace lifted his feet from the table enough for Gabe to finish scooping the crumbs off it. "It looks great, Martha."

"Fuck you," Gabe spat, but he had to admit it was funny. He'd never cared this much what a woman thought of him—or in this case, his place—and he wasn't sure what to make of it.

"Who's Martha?" Manny asked him.

Gabe shook his head at having to clarify the joke that wasn't even his. "Stewart."

"Oh," Manny said, pointing at Jace. "Nice one."

"Get it all out now," Gabe warned, "because if you fuckers even think of doing anything—" A knock interrupted Gabe's threat, so he just gave his friends a two-fingered "I'll be watching you" gesture and headed for the door.

Gabe always thought it was as corny as it was awkward for people to say, "Hey, you," but that is exactly what came out of his mouth when he saw Rachel standing in the hall. She looked casual in black leggings that stopped just above her ankle and a long burgundy sweater that came just below her ass. Gabe thought it was unfortunate that she'd chosen to cover such a perfect area.

She looked beautiful despite the comfortable outfit choice, and Gabe found himself thinking how she'd look beautiful in anything. She certainly looked beautiful *without* any clothes on. "Everyone's in the man cave," he said, gesturing for her to walk down the foyer hallway.

Walking beside her, he had the urge to put a hand on her back, or anywhere on her really, but somehow he managed to restrain himself. When they got into the family room, two pairs of eyes transferred their attention from the game to Rachel. It made Gabe feel more uncomfortable than it seemed to make Rachel feel.

Jace waved at her from the couch and told her it was nice to see her again. She gave him a friendly smile back and said hello.

"This is Manny," Gabe said, causing Manny to ask why wasn't important enough to be introduced by his last name.

Manny lit up when Rachel told him she knew it anyway. "Manny 'Big Quick' Gomez," she said. "You're a Premiers legend. It's so great to meet you."

Manny rose to shake Rachel's hand and then settled back into his spot on the couch.

Gabe told her to make herself comfortable and headed to the kitchen to get her a drink. He returned with Rachel's beer and sat down next to her. "Rachel's in the city doing an article.

It's like a behind-the-scenes sort of thing about teams on the east coast," Gabe said to Manny.

"You're a reporter?" he asked her, and Gabe realized that he hadn't actually said what Rachel did for a living.

"Yeah, nothing too exciting yet. Mostly little stories here and there."

"Okay, okay," Manny replied. "This is cool. Let me know if you wanna interview me. I'd be happy to help. I've got a winning personality."

"But clearly not a modest one," Gabe said.

Rachel laughed and thanked Manny politely. "That's actually what I wanted to discuss with you," Rachel said, turning to Gabe. "I had another idea. It's a bit different than the original one, but it'll allow me to stay in one place instead of hopping from city to city."

Gabe felt his smile brighten. "You wanna focus on only me, don't you?"

"And *I'm* the one who's conceited." Manny laughed.

"There's no way she wants to focus on you," Jace said. "That'd be the most boring article in like...the history of articles."

"That was eloquent," Gabe said.

Jace shrugged. "It's the truth. No one would want to read a whole article about you, let alone write one. You always think that things are about you."

"Actually," Rachel said, "I was thinking that—"

"Don't say it," Jace and Manny said nearly in unison, and Gabe could almost feel how scared they were at what Rachel was about to say. It was in direct contrast to Gabe's growing excitement.

"I was thinking," Rachel began slowly, "that an article that included Gabe might be—"

"The worst idea ever?" Manny said.

"The biggest mistake of your career?" Jace added.

"Shut up and let the woman speak," Gabe said. He was already standing in celebratory anticipation. He would not let a bum knee keep him from jumping up and down when Rachel said she was going to write an article about him.

Rachel smiled, clearly amused at their banter. "I was thinking an article about retired athletes from the four major sports would be interesting to a lot of sports fans. People are used to seeing their favorite sports figures in headlines while they're still playing, but after they retire, typically fans don't have as much insight into their lives. I thought it would be fun to give people a glimpse into what life is like beyond the buzzer, so to speak."

Manny looked incredulous. "And you thought it was a good professional decision to include Gabe in an article that's supposed to be 'fun' and 'interesting'?" he said, using air quotes to emphasize how ridiculous he thought the idea was.

"You guys are assholes," Gabe said, but he couldn't help but laugh.

"I do," Rachel replied with a nod. "My plan is to focus on athletes of different ages and places in their lives. Gabe's still young, and he retired at the height of his career. He doesn't have a wife or kids or anything tying him down. The possibilities of what he could do with his time are endless."

"And yet he's chosen to do nothing," Jace said. "What could be more interesting than that?"

"I do stuff," Gabe defended.

Jace looked at him, obviously knowing there was no way that Gabe would reveal that he'd taken over the club.

"You're helping all of those animals," Rachel said. "I think people would be surprised to know that."

"I know I was surprised," Jace said, causing Gabe to mouth a *Fuck you* at him. At least Gabe had thought to adopt two kittens after telling Rachel about his latest way of giving back. It made him feel better knowing his claim about helping animals wasn't a complete lie. The fact that he was somewhat allergic to cats had no bearing on his decision to suddenly share his place with Tom and Jerry—who were no doubt hiding somewhere because of all the company. There was no way he was getting a dog. No. Way.

Gabe managed to avoid any glances toward Manny, who he was sure was wondering what the fuck Rachel was talking about. Thankfully, even if Manny was skeptical, their bro code wouldn't allow him to call Gabe out on it.

Rachel continued. "That's actually what made me think that profiling you first might be a good idea. I saw that commercial with Sarah McLaughlin and all of those sad puppies, and I thought, people need to know everything you're doing for the local community—that your contribution to the Philadelphia area didn't stop when your baseball career ended. I thought I could do kind of like a day in the life of Gabriel Torres kind of thing and follow you around. You know, really see what you do with your time now that it's not devoted to baseball."

Gabe had been so excited at the prospect of Rachel wanting to focus a quarter of the article on him that he hadn't stopped to consider how she'd get her information or what the article might include. It would be more trouble than it was worth to let Rachel see the ins and outs of his daily routine. "That's nice and all," Gabe began, "but to be honest, the guys are right. I'm not that interesting. But I'm sure I could hook you up with some people who are. Manny's got a lot going on actually, like with the ..."

He pointed at Manny, hoping his friend would help him out. Gabe should've known better. "I don't know what he's talking about," Manny said. "Coming here is the most I've done in weeks."

"Well, I for one, think it's a great idea to profile our friend here," Jace said, squeezing the back of Gabe's neck so hard he thought he might pass out.

Obviously sensing Gabe's hesitation, Rachel assured him that she only wanted to include Gabe in the article if he wanted to do it. She didn't want to force him into anything.

"Are you kidding?" Jace said. "Gabe's been waiting for the day when someone would devote pages to him, right buddy?"

Though Jace obviously didn't want Rachel finding out about the club, he also probably knew that Gabe could prevent that from happening. It would just be a huge pain in his ass. Which was exactly why Jace was suddenly on board with the idea.

And since Gabe was never one to back down from a challenge, he found himself giving Rachel a wide smile and saying how he couldn't be more excited. Add that to the list of ridiculous lies he'd told her.

RACHEL

Rachel hadn't been lying when she'd said that it would be like she was one of the guys. She'd watched the second half of the game with Gabe and his friends and had thoroughly enjoyed herself. They'd discussed who they all thought would make it to the finals, and Rachel had easily taken part in the conversation. After Jace and Manny had left, she'd teased Gabe about how awestruck he'd looked while she was interacting with the guys. But he'd simply said that he'd never been more turned on talking about sports before.

"So maybe I'm *not* one of the guys after all," she said, laughing.

"No. You're way hotter than Manny. I promise."

"You're crazy," she said with a shake of her head as she opened Gabe's recycling and put her empty bottle inside.

"And *you're* beautiful." When she turned back around to face him, his normally easygoing expression had transformed into something more serious. She could feel the weight of his stare on her, his eyes heavy with the same desire she felt whenever she thought of him now. "I mean it," he said, moving closer to her.

"You're drunk" was her only reply.

He shook his head. "Uh-uh. No such thing as beer goggles when I've only had three beers. You're gorgeous."

Rachel wanted to roll her eyes but managed to stop herself. Gabe was being incredibly sweet. She didn't know why she felt the need to tease him about the compliment. Though when she thought more about it, she realized it probably had something to do with the fact that she rarely received such overt compliments from the men she'd dated.

Wait, was she *dating* Gabe? They'd had sex once and gone on one date. That hardly qualified as dating. But she found herself wanting more—whatever "more" meant.

When they were in college, Gabe had always been so free with his compliments, and she'd attributed it to his "player" lifestyle, like she was just one more girl he hoped to add to the already long list of women he'd been with. It had been the main reason she'd turned him down so many times when he'd asked her out. She couldn't be some name he'd forget one day. Mainly because she knew she wouldn't forget *him*.

And now years later, their paths had somehow crossed again when they'd run into each other at the Super Bowl afterparty. And then *again* when Rick had said that the lead to the article of her career happened to be in Gabe's town. The universe had thought it was a good idea to throw them together again, and she couldn't pretend she was disappointed in that. She knew even if she and Kellan hadn't run into Gabe that day, she could only avoid telling him she was in town for so long before she eventually called him. And though she hated that her true reason for being in Philly was something she couldn't share with Gabe, she'd done what she could to rectify that by coming up with an article that she would not only actually write, but would hopefully allow her to get some time and money from Rick while she focused on both articles.

"Why are you so nice?" she asked, her head tilting to the side as she placed her hands on the counter behind her.

He lifted an eyebrow at her and slid a hand into the pocket of the white mesh shorts he was wearing. She found herself remembering what was underneath them and had to direct her attention back to his other head. "Um... Because if I wasn't, my mom would find a wooden spoon that reached from Puerto Rico to Pennsylvania and beat my ass with it." Then he smiled this shy little smile that was somehow so *not* Gabe. "And also because I like you," he said. "And for the first time since I met you, I think you like me too."

Rachel felt herself blush at his words. "I always liked you."

Rachel noticed the corner of his mouth turn up as he jerked his head back in surprise. "No way."

"It's true."

"Was it like when kids have a crush on someone in grade school and they tease and torment them to show they care?" Gabe joked.

"I never tortured you. And we hung out once or twice after I interviewed you."

"We did. But you didn't seem all that interested in taking things any further than coffee or lunch or whatever."

Her shoulders lifted into a shy shrug. "I was interested in *you*. I just wasn't interested in being Gabriel Torres's next conquest."

She hadn't meant for her words to sting. But when she saw Gabe try to hide a wince, she regretted saying them. "I'm sorry. That's not what—"

"No, it is," Gabe said quietly. "It's okay though. I deserved that." He brought a hand up to cup her face while he looked into her eyes with his warm brown ones. "But for what it's worth, you were never a conquest. And you certainly aren't now."

"Then what am I?" she asked.

"Someone I enjoy spending time with. Someone who's incredibly beautiful. And smart. Someone I wanna kiss so badly right now it's hard for me to keep using my mouth to speak."

"Then you should probably stop talking and kiss me."

And just like that, his lips were on hers, his solid body pressing against her as she relaxed into him. Her whole body responded to his touch. It seemed like every nerve, every inch of skin was alive with pleasure.

Gabe's hands roamed her body slowly—carefully, as if

he wanted to savor every second of their encounter. It was different from their first time together, which felt rushed and frantic with need. She sucked in a breath when she felt Gabe's mouth on her neck. He remained there for what felt like an eternity because, though she was thoroughly enjoying it, she wanted his mouth on other, more intimate parts of her.

"I love the little sounds you make," Gabe whispered against her skin.

She'd been so focused on what he was doing, she wasn't even aware she'd made any sounds. "Yeah?" she said, more as a moan than an actual word.

He let out a low "mm-hmm" against her throat as he gradually worked his way to her collarbone. He pulled her sweater to the side to gain access to her shoulder, but the shirt didn't stay on for long anyway. Gabe pulled it over her head and set it on the counter behind her, and now kissed the swell of her breasts as he carried her toward what she assumed was his bedroom.

Instinctually, her legs wrapped around his waist as he carried her, though it was more for pleasure than it was to ensure she didn't fall. She was practically writhing against him. She had no idea how he was able to carry her so easily, and though it made her wonder if it bothered his knee, she decided not to ask.

Once inside his room, the two collapsed onto his soft mattress—causing his two new kittens, Tom and Jerry, to finally make an appearance by darting out from under the bed. Rachel and Gabe both laughed softly as they watched the gray furry felines disappear into the hall.

When Gabe's focus returned to her, the weight of his body was a welcome feeling over hers. He wasn't quite resting himself fully on her but was putting enough pressure against her clit to make her wonder if he would make her come from this alone. There were only a few thin layers of fabric between them, and somehow they caused the sensation of his erection to be more powerful. The way the seams of their clothing rubbed her, how thick and fully ready he was as he moved between her legs. His movements were slow, causing a gradual buildup deep inside her that had her aching for him to move faster, thrust harder.

When she could feel her release creeping down her body, she clung on to him harder, sliding her hands down the back of his shorts and digging her nails into the meat of his ass. She knew what Gabe meant when he'd said he'd liked the sounds she made because the raspy and labored groan he let out had her nearly convulsing under him.

"Gabe," she huffed out. "I need you to…" Her brain somehow disconnected from her voice, making her unable to finish the sentence. She was incapable of any coherent thoughts as Gabe's cock continued to stroke her.

"You need me to what?" Gabe asked. His movements had stopped with his words, and his face held concern. But for what, she wasn't sure. "Is this okay? What I was doing? We can… *I* can…"

Oh God. He thought she wanted him to stop or was unsure if she wanted him to keep going. Pulling at the back of his hair, which was slightly damp with sweat, she gave him a sweet smile and guided him toward her for a kiss that was as innocent as Rachel could manage for the moment. But despite its softness, there was a heat to it—an attraction that made her entire body crave him in a way that she'd never craved anyone before. "Yes," she finally said when their lips parted. "This is… God, it's perfect." She wasn't quite sure what could make fooling around with her clothes still on perfect, but Gabe had accomplished it.

"Oh, okay. That's good," he whispered, his shy smile growing wider at her words. "Because I really didn't want to stop."

"Well, that makes two of us," she said before pressing her lips to his again.

But this time was different. The kiss was long and passionate and completely consuming. It held a power that made her lose all sense of time. The only thing that mattered was now. She thought of nothing but Gabe's hands on her and hers on him as she explored all the parts of him she hadn't been sober enough their first time together to pay any attention to. She focused on every freckle, every scar and soft hair. He was quite possibly the sexiest man she'd ever seen naked.

She felt herself submit to him as one of his hands pinned both of hers over her head. She was sure she could get up if she wanted to, but there was no way in hell she was moving right now. Not with Gabe's scruff tickling her neck as he kissed it. And definitely not when his mouth went to her breasts, lavishing each nipple with equal attention.

Somehow there was no rush despite their need for one another, and when Gabe finally sheathed himself in the condom he'd grabbed from the table next to his bed and slid inside her, she nearly came from that feeling alone. She was so full, so ready. And with him seated fully inside her and momentarily still, she could feel how thick he was.

His thrusts were long and slow and had her begging for more. She felt him chuckle against her ear more than she heard it, and she supposed it was because he was enjoying how needy she was. He continued his measured strokes inside her until at last he rolled her onto him so she could set the pace. She was almost embarrassed of how frantic she was as she rode him, but it was Gabe. Somehow she was able to let herself go around him and let go of all her insecurities.

Her hands were on her own chest and then on her clit as she rubbed herself shamelessly toward an orgasm she was certain she'd never be able to replicate alone.

"I'd tell you how hot that is, but I'm pretty sure you already know," Gabe said, his voice low and raw.

Too turned on, she couldn't even respond, and she knew it wouldn't be long before she lost complete control of herself.

"Let me," Gabe said, taking over where she'd left off.

Her hands went to his shoulders and then to his thighs so she could lean back and give Gabe the access he needed. Their labored breaths were practically in sync with one another, and she wondered if Gabe was as close as she was. A few seconds later, her body shook with her release, and as she tightened around him, Rachel could feel Gabe follow behind her. Their moans and choppy breaths mingled in the heat between them.

And now that Rachel had gotten to thoroughly enjoy Gabriel Torres, she was sure no one else would ever match up to him.

CHAPTER ELEVEN

GABE

"You look very formal," Gabe said. He'd never thought a woman looked so hot in a suit before, but the way the navy skirt hugged Rachel's toned legs had him remembering what it felt like to be between them. She took off her jacket and hung it carefully on the tall chair at the high-top table, revealing a white blouse that was just sheer enough to allow him a glimpse of the bra she wore underneath. "I feel underdressed."

Rachel placed her MacBook on the table and opened it. Then she set a legal pad and pen beside it. "I felt like I should be professional since we'll be discussing the specifics of your part of the article. Sometimes I'm more efficient if I dress like I'm going to work, even when I'm not." Looking slightly embarrassed, she laughed. "That probably makes no sense."

"No, I get it. It's like when people who work from home take a shower and get dressed before they start their day. Because staying in their pajamas would make them want to lie around instead of work."

"Yes," Rachel said, smiling. "Exactly like that." She started up her computer as the waitress came over to get their drink order.

Gabe ordered a pitcher of margaritas for them and some chips and guacamole to start, but before the server left, it occurred to him that maybe Rachel wouldn't want to drink. "Is that okay?" he asked. "I figured we can't have Mexican food without margaritas, but I know you're technically working, so if you don't want to drink..."

"No, a margarita or two's fine. You may have to finish the rest of the pitcher on your own though."

"Not a problem," Gabe assured her before thanking the server, who then left to grab their drinks.

She returned a few moments later with a pitcher and two glasses for them. Pouring the first of their drinks, she told them their appetizer would be out soon.

"Okay," Rachel said. "Let's get started." She offered Gabe a small smile, but he couldn't shake the feeling that she seemed a little... distant.

"Sounds good." Gabe wasn't exactly sure what they'd be discussing when Rachel had suggested that the two of them meet to go over the focus of the article, and he hadn't asked any questions, figuring that Rachel would lead the conversation.

"I was thinking we could try to come up with some ideas of things we could do together. I think once I see what you fill your time with, I'll have a better idea of what the focus of the article will be."

Gabe nodded, unsure if her comment required him to reply. When she didn't say anything else, he said, "Okay. Tell me what you need from me. I'm happy to help."

"Well, I already know you've been helping animals, but you said you haven't volunteered at a shelter yet, so I thought maybe we could find one and I could take some pictures of you there, and—"

"Oh, I actually went to one recently. I can tell you about it because I'm not sure when I'll get to go back. They said that they had other people waiting to volunteer, too, and since it was such a rewarding experience, I want to make sure other people get to help out. I think there are some high school kids who need community service hours or something." Gabe knew he was rambling. And he wasn't sure where he'd even come up with this story, but he was glad he had. Going to an animal shelter with Rachel was not something he wanted to do. It was bad enough he'd been fostering two animals that he couldn't pet without sneezing uncontrollably and having to wash his hands constantly.

Rachel moved her laptop to the side so the server could put their chips down. When the woman asked if they were ready to order, Rachel told them they hadn't even looked at the menu yet. "What's good here?" Rachel asked Gabe once the server had left.

"Pretty much everything. I've been coming to this place for years and have never had anything I didn't like."

She nodded, and when the waitress returned a few minutes later, Rachel ordered the chipotle chicken salad. "I'm hoping it'll be less messy than some of the other things," she said to Gabe after he told the server his order. "I haven't even had this computer for a month. Knowing me, I'll spill sauce on the keyboard or something." She picked up a chip and popped it into her mouth, chewing thoroughly before speaking again. "Okay, where were we?" she asked, and Gabe hoped she'd forgotten that she'd been trying to get him to go to an animal shelter.

"Oh yeah, the shelter," she said, writing the words *Volunteer Work* on the top of her paper and then the word

Shelter below with a line connecting the two. "I think it'd be best if I could see you working at one rather than just hear about it. It's something people would want to learn about you, not to mention it would confirm what a good guy you are."

"What?" Gabe said, pretending to be offended. "I'm a total badass."

She looked doubtfully at him.

"It's true. I barely ever go the speed limit, and I've eaten right before swimming more times than I can count. Oh, and I've already had two margaritas," he added, pouring himself another drink. Then he topped her drink off before setting down the pitcher.

She rolled her eyes good-naturedly and shook her head.

"What? You needed a refill."

Ignoring his comment, she drew two more lines from the heading. She wrote *Hospital Visits* at the end of one line and looked up at him expectantly. "So what other volunteer work do you do?"

Luckily, he had something to add that was true. "I'm pretty involved in a baseball camp for inner-city kids, but that's not until March. But when it starts, you're welcome to tag along."

She added *Baseball Camp* to her outline before looking back across the table at him. "That's a good start. Now why don't you tell me a little bit about how you spend your free time. Like what does Gabe do for Gabe? Do you golf with friends, or ...?" She waited for him to plug in an idea of his own.

"I golf every now and then, yeah. I'm pretty horrible though. I blame it on the fact that baseball's always occupied my time during the nice weather. I think I'll need some more time off to improve my game."

Rachel laughed. "Okay, so we won't put golf. But you hang

out with some guys, I'm sure. What do you usually do? Where do you go?"

Gabe's eyes bounced around the restaurant as he tried to come up with something that didn't involve the club because now that he'd been running it, he and his buddies rarely went anywhere else. He missed having a chance to bullshit with his friends who didn't belong to the Players' Club, and now that Rachel was in the picture, he'd have even *less* time. But that, he didn't mind at all. He wished he could be with her more, so now that he thought about it, maybe Rachel profiling him wouldn't be such a bad idea. His only real concern was what might happen if he had to attend to club business when he had a commitment with her.

"The usual," he finally said with a shrug. He almost laughed at how dumb his answer was, considering how long it had taken him to come up with it. "We go to each other's games, hang out at local bars, stuff like that."

"Which ones?" She hadn't written anything down but was still holding the pen, her eyes fixed on him as she waited for a response.

"What?"

"The bars. Which bars do you usually go to when you hang with your friends?"

"Oh. Um... Duke's and The End Game sometimes." When she still hadn't written anything down, he asked her if she probably should.

"Yes," she answered, grabbing her pen and writing. "Duke's and The End Game. Got it. Are those both sports bars?"

"The End Game is. Duke's is more of a local hangout."

She nodded as she recorded what he'd said. "Do people bother you and the other athletes when you're at these sorts of places?"

Gabe looked around and then back at Rachel. "No one's bothered us tonight," he said as if that was a sufficient explanation. "A lot of times people don't even recognize me."

She settled back in the booth, crossing her arms over her chest. "But I'd think that a bunch of famous people hanging around together would draw a crowd. Because if someone recognizes just one person, then they start to recognize the rest. You know what I mean?"

Rachel's point was a valid one. It's the main reason Mike had started the club to begin with and why so many guys joined. "I guess we usually get lucky," he answered. "Or we've been going there so long, people are used to it."

"Who do you usually hang out with? Former teammates? I know you're good friends with Jace and Ben, but they're not around for a lot of the year."

Gabe wondered where her interest in his friends had come from. He couldn't imagine that readers would care much about who he ran with. "Some old teammates, some other guys I've come to know over the years." And that was the truth. Before he'd started going to the Players' Club regularly, he had a group that would get together from time to time, but they'd mostly hung out at games or events they all attended. Rachel was right to think it was tough for athletes to socialize in public.

"Like...?"

"Are you asking for people's names?" Gabe didn't mean for his question to sound accusatory, but he could hear that it did. He didn't know how comfortable other people would be if they were mentioned in the article. Sure, all of them were used to having stories written about them—good, bad, or indifferent, but Gabe didn't know how he felt about being the *reason* for it. "You'll check with them first before they're included in the story, right?"

"Of course," Rachel assured him. "And I don't even know that I *will* include them. But I want to give everyone a picture of the whole Gabriel Torres, and that includes all aspects of your life. Knowing about your friends will help me portray who you really are when you're not on the field."

Gabe spun his water between his hands before taking a sip and sliding it over to the side.

Seeming to sense his unease, Rachel spoke. "You don't have to give me names if you'd rather not."

"No, no, it's fine," he replied. Rachel had an article to write, and if speaking to some of his friends might help her do it, he didn't want to make things more difficult for her. He knew his concern was probably unfounded; the guys would likely be happy to help out as long as it was before the season began. "Jay Walker and Bryce Clark mostly. And I'm sure I'll be hanging around with Manny more now since he's retired too." He watched her write the names before he asked what she was going to use her computer for.

He was relieved when the question made her laugh. "I don't know actually. I always bring it to interviews, even though most of the time I don't end up using it for anything." Then she picked up her glass and took a sip of her margarita. "Drinks should be mandatory at all business meetings."

Gabe enjoyed the way her pink lips pressed softly on the glass, leaving behind a trace of lipstick, and he tried not to think about what they would feel like wrapped around his cock. Thankfully, the server setting down their meals brought him out of his dirty daydream.

To make room for the food, Rachel closed her laptop and slipped it into the bag beside her. "What else can we discuss?"

she asked once the waitress left.

Gabe thought for a moment as he ate a bite of one of his steak tacos. "How about you?"

A look of confusion flashed across Rachel's face. "Me?"

"Yeah," he replied, wiping his face with his napkin. "You know way more about me than I do about you."

"Well . . . you're the focus of the story."

He shrugged. "Yeah. But I don't have to be the focus of *everything* right now."

Smirking, she raised an eyebrow. "That may be the only time I ever hear you say that."

"Come on," he said. "I'm being serious. Tell me a little bit more about yourself."

Leaning against the back of the booth, she seemed to relax. Her shoulders were open and confident as smoothed the napkin on her lap. "What do you want to know?"

Everything. Gabe couldn't think of anything he *didn't* want to know about Rachel. "Tell me something you've never told anyone," he said.

RACHEL

Rachel didn't know what exactly she'd been expecting Gabe to ask, but it wasn't that. And since she was a reporter, that was pretty impressive. She thought hard for a moment before saying, "I have no idea how to answer that."

"I mean, it doesn't have to be some deep, dark secret or anything. Just something that makes you *you* that no one knows about." Gabe smiled, revealing dimples she'd somehow managed not to notice until now. Though she didn't know how that was possible when they seemed to light up his whole face. "Would it help if I gave you an example?"

"Probably."

"Okay." As he thought, Gabe's eyes went to the ceiling before settling back on her. "Sometimes when I'm out, I put in earbuds so no one talks to me. Most of the time I'm not even listening to anything."

"Seriously?" Rachel laughed.

Gabe nodded, but his eyes flashed with embarrassment.

"You're so friendly though. And social. I'm surprised."

He shrugged, his expression sobering a bit. "I know. I've been told I have one of those faces that people want to talk to. Like I'm inviting them to tell me all about their lives." He ran a hand over his forehead and shook his head. "Does it make me sound like an asshole for not wanting to talk to people?"

"No, not at all. It makes you sound...normal actually. I can't blame you for wanting to have some time to yourself. People probably bother you constantly."

"Sometimes. A lot of the people who talk to me randomly don't even realize who I am. At least I don't think they do because they never mention it. But if I'm at the store or something, people will give me suggestions on salad dressings or tell me about their divorce." Laughing, he shook his head. "It's awkward."

"I bet. I must have a resting bitch face because strangers never talk to me."

"You definitely don't have one of those." Gabe chuckled softly, but his expression sobered quickly. When his eyes locked on hers, she thought she might get lost in them. "You're beautiful, and kind, and sincere."

"Thank you," she said. "You're sweet."

"I'm honest."

She tried to ignore how his last comment made her feel because it reminded her that even though she wanted to share the truth with Gabe, she couldn't. "I guess it's my turn," she said, and Gabe leaned toward her a little more. "The day in college when I interviewed you… I was glad Jace couldn't make it."

Gabe's eyes narrowed. "What do you mean?"

"I was nervous about interviewing some hotshot athlete who all the girls loved."

"And you were relieved when you got the opposite of that?"

"Stop. That's not what I meant," she said, but she could tell he was teasing her. "I was worried he'd be some arrogant jerk or something who couldn't be bothered to respond to my questions. But then you showed up, and you looked genuinely thrilled to be there." As she spoke, she remembered a younger Gabe, his eyes twinkling with excitement as he sat down in front of her. "You were such a goof. But it put me more at ease, which I appreciated."

Gabe's lips quirked up like he considered saying something but decided against it.

"So I guess that's the thing I've never told anyone," she said, her hands locking together on the table before stilling completely. "I was glad it was you. I'm *still* glad it's you."

Gabe's eyes looked heavy, and he took a deep breath in before taking her hand in his. "I'm glad it was me, too," he said. Then there was a silence between them, and Rachel wondered which one of them would feel the need to fill it first. She was just happy to stare at him. As far as she was concerned, words weren't needed.

"Can we shift this business meeting to a date?" Gabe asked, making Rachel smile.

"I guess," Rachel replied. "Why?"

Gabe leaned onto his forearms, moving closer to Rachel. "Because I'm wondering whether I get to kiss you at the end of the night."

Rachel could feel her cheeks heat, and though her eyes darted down for a moment, his didn't leave her. "You don't have to wait till the end of the night," was all she said. With that, they both leaned in, their lips meeting under the dim light above the table. And somehow in a crowded restaurant, it became only the two of them.

CHAPTER TWELVE

RACHEL

"I'm excited to watch you with the dogs," Rachel said as she sank back into the seat of the Uber that Gabe had called to take them to the animal shelter where he said he'd started volunteering about a week ago. She was happy that her words weren't a complete lie. She *was* excited to get to spend time with Gabe and watch him play with puppies. What could be cuter than that? But she was also slightly worried that it was taking her off track.

There was a finite amount of time for her to get this story, and hanging out in an animal shelter wasn't going to get her closer to finding out more about who was running the club. But she'd have to be patient and hope it paid off. Looking over at Gabe, she watched him run a hand through his short hair.

"Yeah, I'm excited too," he said in a tone that was utterly devoid of excitement.

Her brow furrowed. "Is today a bad day? You seem a little . . . off."

Gabe looked over at her. "No, no, today's fine. Sorry. Guess I'm a little nervous about being interviewed," he said with a shy smile she hadn't seen on him before.

"Really? You always seem to love being the center of attention."

"I do … sometimes." Gabe turned to look out the window for a second before returning his gaze to her. "I guess I'm complicated," he said with a smirk that was more signature Gabe.

"I'll be sure to detail your complexity in my article," she joked.

He returned her smile, but it seemed strained.

Rachel put a hand on his arm and squeezed. "I'm kidding. I know there's a lot to you beyond the professional baseball player. That's what I want to show people. That behind the cocky exterior is a real man who has concerns and hopes and fears just like everyone else."

"What if I like people only seeing the cocky exterior?" he asked.

Rachel bit the inside of her cheek. She'd been so excited when she'd thought of writing an article on retired athletes and including Gabe, she'd kind of bulldozed him with the idea. She hadn't given him much opportunity to refuse, and now that she saw how nervous he seemed, she was sorry for it. The last thing she wanted was to stress him out. Rubbing her thumb back and forth on his arm, she smiled warmly. "If you're not up for this, Gabe, it's no problem. It's not too late for me to find someone else. I need to find three others anyway. I enjoy spending time with you, and this allowed me to have the best of both worlds. But I don't want to make you miserable just so I can get a story."

Gabe sighed and returned her smile. "I'm not miserable. And I like spending time with you, too."

"You sure?"

"I'm sure." He patted the hand she still had on his arm. "I

just don't like the idea of someone putting their tongue all over you, even if it's only a dog."

They laughed for a moment before their gazes locked and held for a heated moment. Rachel felt warmth flood her body as she stared into the deep brown orbs that always looked at her so fondly.

"Here we are," the driver said, causing them both to jolt out of the trance they'd been caught in.

Rachel looked out the window at the Center City Animal Shelter they'd pulled up in front of. It was a dank, gray building that looked like it was in desperate need of some TLC. A woman emerged holding four dogs on leashes. Rachel's door opened suddenly, startling her.

Gabe held out a hand to her. "Ready?"

Putting her hand in his, she got out of the car. They approached the building with their fingers interlaced until they reached the door. Gabe pulled it open and gestured for her to go in first. Inside, there was another door that they needed to be buzzed through. Once they made it all the way inside, Rachel found herself at a reception desk, where an older blond woman sat smiling at them.

"Can I help you?" the woman asked.

Gabe moved in front of Rachel so he could speak to the woman. "Uh, yeah. My name is Gabe Torres. I'm here to volunteer."

Rachel was a little surprised the woman didn't know Gabe already, but chalked it up to the woman perhaps not having been working when Gabe had volunteered before.

"Of course! Welcome," the woman gushed. "I didn't recognize you without your uniform on," she said, an obvious element of flirting infused into her tone. "I'm Sheila. I'll call for Micah to come give you a tour."

"Thank you," Gabe said as he turned back to face Rachel.

"Haven't you been here before?" Rachel asked.

"What?"

"You told me you'd been volunteering. Why would you need a tour of a place you've been?"

Gabe's eyes darted around before landing back on her. "I, um, I was pretty much still in the planning phase of volunteering. This was one of the ones I looked into helping out at, but I haven't actually been here yet."

"So you haven't been to this shelter yet?"

"Nope." He shrugged. "I figured it would be fun to start at a new place together."

Rachel smiled at Gabe's cuteness. "Do you think you'll keep any of them?" she asked.

"Any of what?"

Rachel couldn't help but laugh at how weird Gabe was being. "The dogs."

"Oh. Right. The dogs. No, no, I wouldn't be a very good dog owner. I'm not home enough to take care of them well, and I also didn't want to choose only one. It might make the other dogs feel bad. Plus, my building doesn't allow them. They only made an exception for the fostering since I wasn't keeping them there permanently. I thought sending them somewhere they could find good homes would be better."

"Oh, okay. That makes sense. I guess." It *didn't* make a whole lot of sense to Rachel, but who was she to judge?

Micah came up, a smiling guy who looked like he was in his early twenties and had curly blond hair. "Hi, guys. Ready to get to work?" he asked as he rubbed his hands together.

"Yup. Totally. Can't wait," Gabe said as he quickly followed Micah.

Rachel trailed behind them, wondering what she'd gotten herself into.

GABE

Gabe was trying—and failing—to pretend he wasn't making all this shit up as he went along. Rachel had so many questions, and it was stressing him out. He should've expected it. She was a journalist, after all. He'd *meant* to volunteer once or twice before she tagged along, but he'd been so busy with things at the club, he hadn't had any time to follow through on it.

Micah bopped along in front of them, pointing out the different places where the animals were housed and cared for. He was so young and carefree. Gabe hated him. It wasn't helping Micah's case that he kept directing all his attention to Rachel. Gabe wanted to lather him in peanut butter and lock him in with the aggressive dogs he'd seen earlier.

"And this is where you'll be working today," Micah said enthusiastically as he used his keycard to unlock a door.

Gabe walked in to see a bunch of deep tubs and tall tables. A few people were working on dogs, clipping their nails and combing matts out of their fur.

"We've chosen a few of our gentler dogs for you guys to wash. Janice over there," Micah said as he gestured at an older woman with graying hair, "will help you. But it's pretty self-explanatory. I'll bring a dog out for each of you. You'll bathe them and then hand them off to the groomers who will do the rest. Sound good?"

No, it sounds close to my worst nightmare. In theory, Gabe liked dogs. In reality, he was scared to death of them. He was hoping the shelter workers would have them clean out kennels or something. Anything that didn't involve him having to touch the dogs. But this was up close and personal, and he wasn't into it. Not that he could tell anyone that. As far as Rachel knew, he'd been running a doggy and kitty hostel out of his place for months. There was no way he could now tell her that he couldn't so much as pet a dog without breaking into a cold sweat. "Yeah," Gabe said, his voice sounding strangled so he coughed to clear it. "Sounds great."

"Sounds good to me too." Rachel was practically bouncing on her tiptoes.

Micah smiled and clapped his hands together. "Excellent. Then I'll go grab the pups and be right back. Janice will show you where the aprons are." He turned and left, the heavy door closing behind him.

"This is awesome," Rachel gushed. "I thought they'd have us doing something gross. But this will be fun. They must not want to scare off the famous athlete by making you do grunt work."

Gabe didn't tell her would've preferred "grunt" work. The two of them approached Janice, who showed them where the rubber aprons were and briefly showed them what to do. "It's pretty straightforward. Micah won't bring any of the tough cases for your first time, so there's no need to worry."

Gabe opened his mouth to reply but was interrupted by the sound of the door opening and two dogs coming in. Eyeing them warily, Gabe stood rooted to his spot on the ground. The dogs bounded over—literally bounded, since they were enormous.

"This is Bandit," Micah said as he looked down at the

dog on his right. "He's a border collie. Super friendly." Micah handed Bandit's leash off to Rachel.

She leaned down to pet Bandit, who seemed to be instantly taken with her. He trotted to the tubs beside her, climbed up the steps, and hopped into the tub with no problems.

"And this is Torque." As if on cue, the dog yanked on his leash. "He's a puller but very friendly. He doesn't love the water, but he won't bite or anything."

That wasn't the most reassuring statement Gabe had ever heard. Hesitating a second, Gabe finally reached out and took the leash. As if sensing a shift in power, Torque yanked and nearly pulled Gabe off his feet. "What kind of dog is he?"

"He's a mutt. He's squat and strong like a pit bull, but his coloring looks most like a shepherd. There also may be some hound in there."

Gabe nodded and stared down at the creature below him. Torque looked back, his mouth stretched wide and tongue hanging out as if he were mocking Gabe. "Come on, boy," Gabe cajoled as he attempted to pull Torque toward the tubs. The dog sat down and refused to move.

"He's a stubborn thing. Won't be a problem once you get him in the tub, but getting him in there is tough sometimes. You may have to pick him up and put him in there."

"Pick him up?" Gabe nearly yelled the words. There was no way he was bending down and putting his face near this dog's teeth and picking up this beast. Nah-uh. No way.

"Yeah." Micah looked over Gabe's shoulder and smiled. "Want me to do it for you?"

Gabe turned to see what Micah was looking at. It was Rachel, soaping up Bandit as she stole glances at Gabe. He couldn't let Micah carry Torque to the tubs. How would he ever explain that to Rachel? "Nah, it's cool. I got him." Taking a deep breath, Gabe squatted down. "Easy, Torque," Gabe said to the dog. "You let me do this without biting my face off, and I'll see about getting you a better name," Gabe whispered as he slid one hand under the dog's stomach and the other behind his back legs.

Gabe moved slowly, trying to ease the dog into the air.

"Wow, man, you must have killer leg muscles to stand up that slowly holding a ninety-pound dog," Micah commented.

Gabe's legs started shaking with the exertion, but finally he was standing up straight. He carried the dog in what felt like slow motion over to the tub and gingerly put him down. Looking over at Rachel's setup, Gabe noticed that there was a place to fasten the dog's leash to keep him still. He attached it and then turned the water on.

From there it was pretty easy. Torque thought it was fun to shake the water off himself every three seconds, but it could've been worse. He could've tried to maim Gabe. Instead, the dog sat there looking grumpy as hell as he let Gabe do what needed to be done. When the bath was finished, Gabe unhooked the leash and lifted Torque again. He found himself actually starting to enjoy the dog's company. Until Torque torqued, causing Gabe to stumble and drop him.

The dog was stunned for a split second after he hit the ground, but he recovered quickly, beginning to run around the room like he was a fucking cheetah. All the other dogs in the room went wild as Torque sped around. Gabe tried to catch him, but it was like trying to catch a greased pig. He wanted to step on Torque's leash to stop him but was worried he'd accidentally break the dog's neck. That's all this day fucking needed.

"Gabe, you go that way, and I'll go this way. We'll try to corral him," Rachel yelled over the yipping and howling that reverberated through the room.

Gabe did as she said, and they closed in slowly on Torque. Finally, when they were within grabbing distance, Gabe lunged for the marauding dog. But Torque, in a move that would've impressed a few football players, faked one way before juking back and running through Gabe's legs, causing his knees to buckle and sending him crashing to the floor.

Lying on his back, Gabe stared up at the ceiling for a minute. His bad knee twanged with discomfort, but he didn't think he'd done any major damage.

"Oh my God, are you okay?" Rachel asked, alarm clear in her tone as she kneeled beside Gabe and let her eyes rove over his body. It was obviously so she could see if he was injured, but he tried to convince himself she was checking him out all the same.

"Yeah, I think so," Gabe replied as he pushed himself to a sitting position. He was about to stand when he felt hot breath on his cheek. He panned slowly to his right and looked straight into the face of Torque. Just as Gabe was about to recoil from the mentally unhinged canine, Torque's giant tongue rolled out and licked Gabe across the mouth.

Gabe jerked his head back and wiped his mouth with a hand as Rachel laughed. "Aw, he likes you," she said.

Gabe wished he could've said the feeling was mutual.

CHAPTER THIRTEEN

RACHEL

Even when they'd gone back to Gabe's after the animal shelter debacle, Rachel was still having a hard time not laughing at the mental image of Gabe looking agitated while getting licked to death by a giant teddy bear of a dog. Despite the ordeal, Gabe had insisted they stay and finish out the time they'd promised the shelter, and he'd tried to put on a brave face, but it was clear he couldn't wait to get out of there.

He'd invited her back to his place to hang out and order takeout, which she'd been all too happy to agree to. While it had been nice spending time with him at the shelter, that had been for her article. Now she'd get to spend time with Gabe simply because she wanted to.

When they'd gotten back to his place, Gabe had excused himself to shower. He'd offered her the shower in his second bathroom, but she hadn't rolled around on the ground with a wet dog and also didn't relish the thought of putting the same clothes she'd worn to the shelter back on afterward. She'd survive a couple hours until she got home.

Though he'd been trying to mask it, it had been obvious that Gabe was favoring one leg over the other. She knew about his injury but wasn't sure how badly he'd rehurt it. She'd asked him about it, but he'd shrugged it off. Hopefully the warm water would help.

Rachel wandered around his living room, unsure what to do with herself. She went over to the coffee table where a bunch of remotes sat, but there were at least five of them and she had no idea what any of them did, so she decided to wait for Gabe to turn on the TV. She let her eyes drift over his place. It wasn't the first time she'd been there, but it was the first time she'd really gotten to give the place a thorough once-over. It was very Gabe. All comfy couches, soft rugs, and sports memorabilia on the walls. The floor plan was open concept, the living room running into the dining room, which was set off from the kitchen only by an island.

She walked over and slid onto a stool and waited for Gabe, reaching her hand out to pet one of the cats who was walking across his counter. But as her hand landed on the kitten, it bolted, knocking some paperwork off the countertop and onto the floor. "Damn it," she said, her tone hushed as she began picking up the papers and trying to get them back in some sort of order that resembled how they'd been before the cat had sent them flying through the air.

But as she did, her eyes landed on a piece of paper on the island. She tilted her head so she could read it. It was a bank statement, which was absolutely none of her business, so she began to tear her gaze away when she noticed the name on top: Helping Hands. *What the hell is that?* If Gabe was getting a bank statement for a company, he'd have to have some fiscal stake in said company. But in all the time they'd spent together—over all the times they'd discussed how he spent his time—he'd never mentioned being a part of a nonprofit.

Rachel reminded herself that there was probably a very logical explanation—one that she could easily find out if she just asked him.

"Hey, what do you feel like eating?" Gabe walked around the corner, rubbing a towel over his damp hair. Rachel couldn't stop her eyes from raking over his body as he wore gray sweatpants that sat low on his hips and a tight blue Premiers T-shirt. His biceps flexed as he toweled off his hair. Rachel had never wanted to be a scrap of terry cloth so badly in her life.

Gabe came around behind her, rubbing a hand along her back as he passed, and went into the kitchen. Walking over to the other side of the island, Gabe pulled open a drawer and withdrew a stack of takeout menus. "These places are all pretty close. Any of them look good?" As he spread the menus out, his eyes locked on the bank statement.

Rachel studied him for his reaction. The widening of his eyes was the only immediate physical response, but he slid his hand over the paper and pulled it toward him as his other hand moved the menus around. It reminded her of how a magician might try to distract an audience by using sleight of hand. He pulled the statement off the island and let it drop into the open drawer.

Rachel kept her head bent down as if she was looking at the menu options, but her eyes followed Gabe's movements carefully. All of Rachel's journalistic senses tingled. There wasn't a cell in her body that thought Helping Hands was something Gabe would want to discuss. And now she had to know why.

Gabe rested his forearms on the granite countertop and smiled at her.

That's when she knew she had to get out of there. Because

even though she didn't have any reason to think Gabe was hiding something, her instincts told her differently. And ever since she'd become a reporter, her gut was the one thing she never ignored. She didn't want to spend time with him cuddling up on the couch watching movies and sharing dinner while her mind was focused on the bank statement. She gasped and looked down at her watch with what she hoped was a believable degree of panic etched on her face. "Oh shit. I totally forgot. I have a conference call with an editor in twenty minutes." She rose from the stool and took a step away from the island. "I'm so sorry. It's for another freelance opportunity; I can't afford to miss it."

She hated how easily she lied to Gabe, who looked disappointed yet understanding. "No worries," he said. "I understand. Rain check? Maybe we can get together for something not-article related this week?"

She smiled at him. "I'd like that. I'll text you later, and we can set something up."

"Works for me."

"Great. Talk to you soon then," she said over her shoulder as she went to retrieve her purse and walked toward the door. When she reached out to turn the knob, she felt the heat of a presence behind her. She wanted to melt into it but managed to restrain herself.

An arm reached around her, making her hope it would snake around her waist and pull her back into Gabe's chiseled chest. But instead, his hand grabbed the lock and turned it. "Gotta unlock it first," he said huskily into her ear.

A shiver worked through her. "Is that how doors work? Good to know," she joked, hoping it would lighten this moment that felt astoundingly sexually charged.

"Glad I could help." He must have taken a step back because the warmth at her back disappeared. "See you later, Rach."

She glanced quickly over her shoulder and offered a sly smile to turn the tables on him a little. "Can't wait, Gabe."

Two hours later, Rachel sat on her stiff couch with a blanket over her legs and her laptop resting on top. She'd been researching Helping Hands since she got home, but it was such a generic name that literally thousands of search results came up. She'd been painstakingly clicking through each one, but there was nothing Gabe had a clear connection to. And he'd have to have a connection if he was receiving their bank statements.

That led her to look into the bank that had sent the statement: The Bank of American Fidelity. And that was where things got interesting. It was a small branch that was in Philadelphia. But its website was...odd. Too simplistic, with no clickable links. Rachel had tried to call them, but no one answered and there was no answering service. It just continued ringing until Rachel eventually hung up. Her next step was to place a call to a friend named Jared, who had a way with computers and a loose moral code. She told him what she knew, and within thirty minutes he'd called her back with the information that let her know she'd found something important.

As it turned out, the Bank of American Fidelity existed under the umbrella of a larger corporation called the Bank of Worldwide Fidelity, which was located in the Cayman Islands. It was all so cliché, it was almost hard to believe. Of course,

Rachel knew that the Cayman Islands were a mecca for people trying to hide funds from the American government, especially since Swiss banks were under investigation and closing at a rapid rate. But it still seemed so... Netflix miniseries. Rachel had a hard time believing that Gabe would be using an offshore bank. It reeked of criminal behavior that he'd never demonstrated he was even remotely capable of. But the fact that he obviously hadn't wanted her to see the statement plagued her mind.

Jared said he could dig around into Gabe's finances if she wanted, but Rachel wasn't willing to go there. Aside from it being illegal, it was also a gross betrayal of his trust, and she didn't want to go that far. Once she got off the phone, she went into her bedroom, where she had papers scattered all over the floor in an intricate web that made sense only to her.

The majority of it dealt with Cole Barnes, but some of his friends were also included. She'd done what research she could on his friends, but she hadn't come up with anything that tied them to the club. Rachel looked over all of it and slumped with the knowledge that it didn't really amount to much. And now, though she hated to think about it, she worried that Gabe might be a member of the club. The bank was the only lead she had—if it even *was* one—and there was no way she could get much further without exploiting that angle at least a little bit.

Taking a deep breath, she retrieved her phone from the living room and called Jared again. When he answered, she said, "If I needed a list of the Bank of American Fidelity's customers, how long would that take you to compile?"

Jared chuckled. "About five minutes. Ten if their security is better than I'm giving them credit for."

She wanted to call him out on his cockiness, but she didn't

have it in her to tease him. "Then I guess I'll check my email in ten minutes."

"You got it. Anything else?"

"No, that's it."

"Okay. Let me know if you change your mind."

"Will do. Thanks."

"No problem," Jared said before ending the call.

Rachel pulled the phone away from her ear and stared at it. She'd gotten the lead she wanted. No, *needed.* But all it made her feel was slightly ill and anxious. *Please let this be worth it,* she thought before walking back out into the living room and waiting ten minutes before opening her email.

CHAPTER FOURTEEN

GABE

Gabe pressed the home button on his phone, making the screen light up. Still no return call from Rachel. He'd called her yesterday and texted two more times when he hadn't heard back. He hadn't wanted to seem desperate, but it wasn't normal for her not to respond, and it made him concerned. After he texted that she was making him worry, and could she please let him know she hadn't been abducted by a religious cult or something, she'd replied that she was fine, just busy, and she'd call the next day.

Well, it was the next day, and she still hadn't called.

It wasn't like Gabe to care about shit like this. Women came and went out of his life constantly, and it had always suited him just fine. Until now.

Until Rachel.

Gabe rolled his eyes at himself. He was being ridiculous. It was only two p.m., and he had things he needed to get done. Rachel was working; he should be too.

It had been an easy couple weeks at the club because it hadn't been open much since the Super Bowl. He tried to open most Saturday nights and had a couple special events, but now that March Madness was only a week away, he had to gear up for being open almost every night for three weeks straight.

Which made Gabe wonder how he was going to manage to spend time with Rachel *and* spend time at the club. It's not that he *had* to be at the club whenever it was open, but it made him feel better if he was. Mike had seemingly always been there, and Gabe wanted to make sure he gave the place the attention its original owner had. He didn't want to fail Mike's legacy. He wasn't sure what kind of excuse he could come up with so that Rachel wouldn't wonder what he was up to. Not that she really had any reason to be suspicious, but she was a journalist. Being suspicious probably came naturally to her.

And then there had been the bank statement he'd left sitting out. He wasn't sure if she'd seen it, or that she would think anything of it if she had. But it made him feel reckless and stupid. That statement was one of the only tangible links to the Players' Club, and if someone made that connection, that would be very bad news for its future. He owed it to all the athletes involved to be more careful.

Which only added to his stress over not hearing from Rachel. Because the longer her article dragged on, the longer he had to keep up a charade that he wasn't at all equipped to pull off. Despite his easygoing jokester demeanor, Gabe was a horrible liar. And it wasn't only that Rachel was a journalist. It was that it was Rachel—a person he legitimately cared about and *wanted* to get close to. But how would that even work?

What if their friendship did turn into more? How would he ever keep this from her in the long-term? He was starting to realize why Mike had been single. The club was already akin to having a spouse. How could Gabe have a girlfriend on top of it?

Not that she'd ever even hinted at wanting to be his

girlfriend. Gabe took some deep breaths and brought himself back from the ledge. Because while there was definite sexual chemistry between them, that didn't necessarily mean she felt any more for him than that. It was no use worrying about something before there was even a hint of it being a possibility. Rachel might finish up her work, head back to New York, and forget all about him.

That thought didn't necessarily make him feel any better, but its finality at least allowed him to focus on the work in front of him.

Then his cell phone rang.

He looked down at it quickly, his heart giving a little leap of hope. When he saw Ben's name on the screen, he tried to ignore the pang of disappointment that caused his shoulders to droop. He answered with a tone he hoped sounded upbeat even though it was forced. "This is weird. My phone says it's Ben calling, but I'm not even sure I know anyone by that name anymore."

"Shut up," came the reply. "Some of us are still in the pros and don't have a lot of free time."

Even though Ben's tone was clearly teasing, the words stung a little. The truth was, Gabe missed baseball and often found himself wondering if retiring had been too hasty of a decision. He might have been able to get a few more solid years in. Instead, he was dealing with purchase orders and vague threats from irate former members. "Please. Your team barely qualifies as professional. Don't you guys have close to the worst record in the league?"

"Because the Premiers were such standouts the past couple seasons," Ben retorted, sarcasm dripping from his words.

"Did you call just to flirt with me, or did you want something?"

Laughter rang out over the phone. "Like I'd flirt with you. I'm way out of your league."

Gabe felt the corners of his mouth turn down. "No, you're not."

"I totally am."

Gabe thought for a moment, pondering what would make Ben out of his league. "Why?"

Ben was silent for a second. "Is this a real conversation we're having?"

"You started it," Gabe replied, even though he knew that wasn't true.

Another laugh huffed through the line. "As mature as ever."

Gabe remained quiet. It was suddenly important to him to hear Ben's explanation, and the only way to get it was to wait him out.

It didn't take long for Ben to break. "Dude, it was a joke."

Gabe knew that. He'd swear up and down that he did. But something still niggled at him. "Maybe."

"What do you mean 'maybe'? If I said it was a joke, it was a joke. I'm not giving any serious thought to dating you."

"A lot of truth is said in jest," Gabe replied.

"Gabriel. Seriously. I know we talked about this before, but I'm really not gay. You do know that, right?"

"That doesn't mean you're not out of my league."

Ben sighed. "What's going on?"

Gabe wasn't sure how to explain it. It was like his entire brain had shifted with one comment, giving light to a truth he'd hidden even from himself. "You and Jace are both settling down. You found people who want to spend the rest of their lives with you. And those people aren't legally insane." Gabe hesitated. Trying to let his mouth say what his brain wasn't totally sure of was difficult. "You guys found good women who love you for who you are. Not because of the money you make or how famous you are, but, like, despite those things. And I haven't."

"That doesn't mean we're better than you, though. It just means we got lucky."

"I don't think you're better people than me, asshole. I volunteer at animal shelters for Christ's sake."

"I heard it was *a* shelter. Singular," Ben said. "And I'm pretty sure that your sudden altruistic mentality has more to do covering your own ass than it does with a desire to better the world."

"Shut up. And stop using words I can't understand. Anyway, I think that maybe you guys are better boyfriend material. Chicks dig me for the short-term, but none of them want to put a ring on it."

Gabe was hoping Ben would laugh, but his voice was serious when he spoke. "But you never wanted that. A lot of those girls would've sold their souls if it would've made you interested in them. The ball's always been in your court. Not theirs."

Pursing his lips, Gabe thought that through. "That's not necessarily true. It's more that the girls I always attract aren't lifers. They're barely one-nighters."

"Is this about Rachel?" Ben asked.

Due to Ben's busy traveling and training sessions, Gabe hadn't been able to do much more than give Ben a very vague rundown of Rachel being back and doing an article on him. He hadn't even gotten to tell Ben about his epic fuckup of saying he was rehoming strays, which had resulted in his getting two small skittish gray balls of fur. Jace must've beaten him to it. But Ben knew Gabe in a way only he and Jace did. "I wanna keep her," Gabe admitted.

"Does she want to be kept?"

Gabe forced out a breath. "No idea."

"Ya thinking ya might wanna ask her?" Ben asked.

"How do I do that? It's awkward as fuck to ask that when you have no idea what the answer's gonna be."

"But that's why you have to ask. How else will you know?"

"Maybe I'll pass her a note in study hall."

"Come on, Gabe. You're a great guy with the best heart of anyone I've ever known. I'm sure she's into you. And if not, that's her loss."

Gabe dropped his head into his hand. "Oh my God."

"What?" Ben asked.

"Did you just give me the token 'high school girl with a crush' speech?"

"Since I don't know what the fuck that is, I'm not sure how to answer your question."

"It's what every high school girl tells her best friend who has a crush. She blows a bunch of candy-coated words up her ass and then puts the disclaimer on the end to make her feel better when the crush slams her heart into a locker."

"Wow. I wasn't aware you spent so much time around high school girls. Do we need to have a talk, Gabe?"

Gabe ignored that remark because . . . gross. "You're the worst at this."

Ben scoffed. "Whatever, man. I'm doing my best to help your sorry ass, but eff it. Yes, I'm out of your league, and you're destined to be a single loser for the rest of your life. How's that?"

"I'm taking you off my Favorites list in my contacts. Keep it up and I'll be forced to unfriend you on Facebook."

A startled laugh escaped Ben before he sobered. "Listen, I admit my advice was probably very after-school special, but the message behind it is valid. Yes, you've attracted a lot of girls in the past who weren't necessarily wife material. But that doesn't mean *you're* not husband material. You're whatever you decide to be. You think I was prepared to fall in love with the girl I was paying to date me? Not a chance. But it happened. And it'll happen for you too, as long as you're open to it. Maybe it'll be with Rachel, maybe it'll be with someone else. But it *will* happen."

"You can't know that. What if I end up getting seventeen more cats and never leave the house because I'm too busy watching reruns of *The Price is Right*?"

"It'll happen, Gabe. You're just going to have to trust me on this one."

And he wanted to. But the reality was, how did someone just *trust* in something like that? And even if it did happen, how would he manage it? But he didn't want to keep going around in circles with Ben, so he said a simple, "Okay."

"Okay? Are you for real right now? After all that building up of your confidence, all I get is an 'okay'?

"Yup. Take it or leave it."

Ben laughed. "I'll take it."

They chatted for a few more minutes about less stressful things before Ben had to go so he could get to practice on time.

After he hung up, Gabe sat back, surveying the sea of paperwork in front of him and knowing there was no way he'd be able to focus on any of it. Instead, he stood, grabbed his keys, and headed toward the one thing he could focus on.

RACHEL

Rachel had been absorbed by the information Jared had sent her for almost twenty-four hours. The bank didn't have very many customers with accounts there, but there were many who routed money from their own bank into the Bank of American Fidelity, specifically the account for Helping Hands. And the people doing so were all professional athletes.

Rachel had then done searches on those athletes to see if they lived locally, or if they commuted to the city with any kind of regularity. And she found that those who did live far enough away to have to fly in, all did so around the same times. Those times seemed to correspond to major sporting events—events a club designed for athletes might celebrate with a fervor only sports-minded people would be capable of.

She'd found her smoking gun.

The only thing that was tripping her up was where Gabe fit into it all. Jared's information didn't dig into what Helping Hands was, nor what Gabe's role in it could be. And while Rachel knew Jared could easily find out, she still couldn't bring herself to go down that road. She was a journalist. She could put the pieces together without someone else doing all the work for her.

But there were so many ways the pieces in front of her *could* fit together, she was struggling to figure out where to start. It felt as though she'd been staring at the array of pictures and jotted notes spread across her bedroom floor for over an hour when she heard an insistent knock at her door.

Her head bolted up as she looked into the hallway. Standing slowly, she tried to imagine who it could be. She took care to make sure her bedroom door was closed before heading out toward the noise. One look through the peephole had her sighing and leaning her head against the door. What the hell was Gabe doing there? And more importantly, how could she avoid letting him in without coming across like an ass?

Rachel took a deep breath in, undid the safety chain and lock, and opened the door.

Gabe stood there looking... pensive. His green Henley looked good on his solid frame, as did the jeans that seemed barely able to contain his thickly sculpted thighs.

Momentarily forgetting that she was supposed to be getting rid of him, Rachel's brain filled with images of Gabe naked and on top of her.

"Am I boyfriend material?"

Gabe's sudden question threw her for a second, mostly because she'd been so lost in looking at him, she hadn't been focused on the fact that he might actually want to hold a conversation. "I'm sorry. What?" she asked.

Gabe pushed his hands into his pockets. "We get along well. I like you. You seem to like me. So I was wondering if this"—he waved between them—"could be... more."

"More?" Rachel needed to hurry up and get with it because she was starting to sound like a moron.

"Yeah. More than friends. More than interviewer and interviewee. Just more."

She was completely unprepared for this conversation. Not because she didn't think of Gabe as potentially being "more," but because she couldn't believe Gabriel Torres would ever want more, let alone say it. Plus, she had a mountain of paperwork that supported an article he might hate her for writing. It was a serious conflict of interest, and she had no idea how to get herself out of it.

But Gabe evidently took her silence for unwillingness because he visibly deflated in front of her. "I guess I should've thought this through better." He looked down at the carpet for a moment before focusing back on her.

The sight of a vulnerable Gabe hit Rachel square in the chest. For a second, thoughts of her article were pushed behind the need to take the sad look of off his face. "I could be open to more."

The smile that lit up his face in response was one of the most magnificent things Rachel had seen in a long time. And she'd seen Gabe's six-pack.

"Maybe I could come in, and we could talk about it?" Gabe said.

Rachel felt her eyes widen in alarm as she unconsciously gripped the door harder.

Gabe noticed. "Holy shit, you don't have a guy in there, do you? Because . . . fuck. That's going to suck."

Despite herself, Rachel laughed. "No. No guy." She opened the door wider. "See? I have a ton of work I've been sorting through for that other freelance article. I guess I'm just . . . protective of my work. I don't like people seeing any of my notes or source material until I'm finished." Rachel was proud of herself for coming up with something that also happened to be true. She'd never thought about it, but she *didn't* like people to see any parts of her stories before she wrote them. Probably because she was worried an offhand comment would make her doubt herself or steer her away from where she wanted the story to go. So there was at least some solace to be found in the fact that she hadn't actually lied.

Gabe, bless his heart, nodded his head like that made all the sense in the world. "Oh. Okay. Well, maybe we can go somewhere else then. Even later. I can wait."

But he shouldn't have to wait. Because even if her words were often straddling the line between fact and fiction, her feelings were one hundred percent real. "You're absolutely boyfriend material, Gabe. The bigger question is if I'm girlfriend material. Especially since I'm only going to be in town for a finite amount of time."

There was an instant look of disbelief on Gabe's face. "Are you crazy? You've been girlfriend material for me since college. And as far as the distance?" Gabe shrugged. "Let's just see how it goes. I don't want it to be an automatic deal breaker."

Rachel knew she should think about it more, but she'd had enough of thinking. One of the reasons she'd turned Gabe down in college because she knew they were starting down very different paths. But now that those paths had crossed again, maybe she should just accept it as some sort of kismet and go with it. "Okay."

"Okay?" Gabe parroted.

"Okay," Rachel confirmed with a smile.

"We should go on a real date then. Off the record."

"I'd like that."

Gabe scratched his chin. "I know you said you were working today. Maybe tomorrow night? I'll pick you up here at six?"

"I'll be here."

"Great."

They stared at each other for a moment. A loss for what to say next turned into getting lost in one another's eyes, and before Rachel could process who had been the first to move,

Gabe's lips were on hers. The soft yet firm press of his mouth set fire through her veins. The now familiar urge to do anything to get Gabe inside of her returned, and Rachel moaned into the kiss and tried to pull Gabe closer.

But instead, Gabe pulled away. "I'm... I... Let's... Jesus, you kissed me stupid." They both laughed before Gabe continued. "I want to make sure you know that what we have is more than just sex. I want to do it right. So let's go on our date tomorrow and then see where the night leads from there."

Rachel wanted to tell him that was the dumbest idea she'd ever heard, especially since they'd been together a few times by that point, but she also didn't want to dissuade Gabe's chivalrous side so she forced herself to breathe evenly before replying. "Sounds good."

Nodding, Gabe took a couple steps back. "All right then. I'll see you tomorrow."

"See you tomorrow."

Gabe smiled before turning and walking down the hall toward the stairs.

"Hey, Gabe," Rachel yelled after him.

He turned and raised his eyebrows.

What she wanted to say sounded stupid now, but nothing more eloquent came to mind, so she was forced to blurt out her thoughts. "I'm excited to be your girlfriend."

"I'm excited, too," Gabe said barely loudly enough for her to hear her. He lifted a hand as a goodbye and made his way down the stairs and out of sight.

Rachel closed the door to her apartment and slumped against the door, wondering how she was going to navigate being Gabe's girlfriend and the reporter investigating him— especially now that she no longer knew which was more important.

CHAPTER FIFTEEN

GABE

Gabe hadn't had much time to think about where he should take Rachel on their date, but he wanted to make sure it was somewhere she'd feel special, appreciated. Now that he was finally getting the opportunity to take her on a real date, he didn't want to fuck it up. He'd made a reservation for a French restaurant in the city that was located on the top floor of a building high enough to see almost the entire Philadelphia skyline, and he hoped she'd like it.

He'd been a little hesitant about trying it out when a friend of his had suggested it after Gabe had asked people for suggestions. Gabe didn't even know if he liked French food—though he liked pretty much everything—and he certainly couldn't speak the language. He'd figured that the menu would be in English, or at least have English translations, but as he stared at the words in front of him, he wasn't sure what the hell he was looking at. Though he didn't think the choices were entirely in French, they weren't in English either. The only word he recognized was "grille," even though the French version had a weird line over it.

Gabe had to admit there were perks to being a local

athlete. He didn't think he ever would have been able to score a table like this otherwise. Apparently the place booked up months in advance. Though Gabe wasn't one to typically use his celebrity status to get him special treatment, he also wanted to make a good impression on Rachel, which he hoped he had since they were seated at a semiprivate table against the window. The sun was setting in the distance, radiating a deep orange through the silhouettes of the buildings. If that didn't scream romance, Gabe didn't know what did. "Do you know what you're getting?" Gabe asked Rachel, who was across from him.

Rachel studied her menu. "Not sure yet. What about you?"

"I'll let you know once I learn to speak French."

Rachel's shoulders fell in what Gabe identified as relief. "Oh, thank God. You don't know what this says either?"

"Not a clue. I figured I'd be able to understand at least some of it."

The two locked eyes and settled back against their chairs as they placed the menus on the table and laughed quietly.

"Should we Google it?" Rachel asked.

Gabe thought for a moment before replying, "Nah. I've got an idea."

When the waiter came back, Gabe admitted that neither of them had any idea what the menu said. The waiter offered to review the menu with them, but Gabe politely declined and asked the waiter instead to bring a few of the chef's recommendations for each of the courses.

"Certainly, sir," he replied before returning his attention to the wine he'd brought them and pouring them each a glass.

Once the server left, Gabe took a sip of the Pinot noir

he'd chosen. "What do you think?" he asked Rachel after she'd tried hers.

"Delicious."

He tried to focus on anything besides the way she licked her lips and how her eyes sparkled in the dim light, but it was a pointless effort. Her beauty wasn't something that he could ignore. Nor should it be, he'd decided. So he let himself take her in completely: the soft curls of her hair, the plunging neckline of her dress. Once his eyes had moved over what seemed like every inch of her that he could see, he spoke again. "Is it bad that the only thing I know how to order is alcohol?"

"Nope," Rachel replied. "I like a man who knows his drinks." And there was that smile that he loved so much. The one that lit up her whole face, giving her these faint creases near her eyes that somehow made her even more attractive.

"Good," Gabe said with a smile. "I like *you*."

The two remained quiet, letting the intimate moment pass between them. It was subtle and unexpected. But like a soft breeze during the heat of the summer, it was also fleeting, interrupted by the waiter returning with some dishes for them to try.

By the time they'd tasted every appetizer and entrée the chef had prepared for them, Gabe was stuffed, and he imagined Rachel was, too. They sampled the desserts that the waiter set in front of them—crème brûlée and some sort of chocolate soufflé, but neither Gabe nor Rachel could eat much of them.

"That was probably one of the best meals I've ever eaten," Gabe said. "And the craziest part is that I have no idea what any of it was." Though the waiter had told them in English what each dish contained and how it was prepared, Gabe had no recollection of any of it. His mouth had more of a memory than his brain, it seemed.

"I'm glad they brought out the duck. I like it, but it's not something you order at just any restaurant, so I rarely eat it."

"I've *never* ordered it," Gabe said. And then, after the two had finished off the last of their wine, he asked, "So what now?"

She shrugged. "You tell me."

Gabe thought for a moment since he hadn't planned anything after this, which he realized now was stupid. He had the night to give Rachel a date she'd remember, and he'd only prepared for the first half of it. "I have an idea," he said, hoping that Joe would answer when he called.

RACHEL

After dinner, Gabe had excused himself to make a phone call. He'd returned with a smile and another bottle of wine that he said they could split once they got to their destination. Whatever he had planned, he was clearly excited for. Gabe paid the bill and then led Rachel downstairs and outside to where the car Gabe called was waiting for them. The driver opened the door for her, and Gabe slid into the seat beside her.

"Are you going to tell me where we're going?" Rachel asked, though she already knew he probably wouldn't.

"When we get there," Gabe said with a smirk, looking pleased with himself. "It's not far."

For the next ten minutes or so, Rachel enjoyed the silent ride to wherever it was they were headed. She snuggled into Gabe's chest when he put his arm around her and let the lights from the street and stores move over her face as she closed her eyes. Gabe's hand rubbed her arm lightly, and she thought how easily she could fall asleep here with him.

When the car came to a stop, Gabe kissed her head and removed his arm from around her. "We're here, sleepyhead."

"I wasn't sleeping," she replied. "I was only resting my eyes. It's not my fault you're so comfortable and you smell so good. You only have yourself to blame."

Gabe laughed as he slid out of the car and extended his hand to help her out too. Rachel took in her surroundings and realized that they were in front of the stadium where Gabe played baseball before he retired. The confused look she gave him should have been enough for him to provide her with an explanation of what they were doing here while the team was still down at spring training. But he simply kept smiling and gestured toward a man who was waiting for them at the entrance.

The middle-aged, slightly balding man greeted Gabe with a warm hug, telling him how great it was to see him again.

"This is Joe," Gabe said. "He's the maintenance manager. Joe, this is Rachel, my beautiful date for this evening."

Though the comment was said somewhat in jest, Rachel knew Gabe meant it. The way he'd been looking at her all night made her feel wanted, admired. She'd chosen the tight, deep-purple dress hoping that he'd like it. And by the way his eyes conspicuously roamed over every visible part of her body at dinner, it seemed she'd chosen wisely. Rachel couldn't take her eyes off him either. She'd never seen him dressed up before, and it was a welcome change. His fitted light-gray suit accentuated his broad shoulders and biceps, and the crisp white shirt he had on under it made his skin appear a shade darker than usual.

"It's so nice to meet you, Rachel," Joe said, ushering

her out of the cool night air. Though for late March, it was unseasonably warm. She probably wouldn't have even been cold if she'd had a light jacket.

Once inside, Joe gave Gabe a set of keys and Gabe told him he'd take it from there. He was quiet as he led them through the halls of the empty stadium. Though Rachel had been in plenty of sports venues throughout her career, she'd never been in one when it was vacant. There was an eerie calm to it that she couldn't explain, as if she were intruding upon a sacred place.

"I feel like a burglar or something," Rachel said. "Like I'll get arrested if someone finds me here." Her voice echoed softly through the cavernous hall along with Gabe's laugh.

"No one's gonna arrest you," Gabe promised. "And for something to be considered burglary, you have to actually break in through force. Joe let us in, so we're good. Take whatever you want," he joked as he opened a door to a small room with light beige carpet, a couch, and a small bar. "Starting with those." Gabe pointed to some clothes that had been folded neatly on the couch. "There's a bathroom here you can change in," he said, gesturing to the closed door to their left. "You'll probably be cold if you stay in your dress."

"We're going outside?" she asked.

"Of course," he said as if her question was a ridiculous one. "You can't go to a ball field and not step foot on the grass. Hopefully the clothes will fit. Sorry if they're a little big."

"I'm sure they'll be fine," Rachel assured him as she held up the pair of blue Premiers warm-up pants that she figured Joe had put out for her. "I'll be out in a few minutes."

Gabe gave her a quick kiss on her forehead and told her he was going to grab a few things and then he'd be waiting for her in the hall.

She changed quickly, putting on the pants, T-shirt, and thick sweatshirt. It felt good to get out of her heels and into flip-flops, which, though a little big, felt a thousand times better than what she'd had on.

"God, you look cute," Gabe said when Rachel came out of the room.

Rachel looked down at the oversized sweatshirt and baggy pants. "Really?"

"Absolutely. None of the guys ever looked that hot in Premiers gear." Gabe laughed at his joke.

"I bet one guy did," she said.

He'd only changed his shoes, rolled up his sleeves, and undone a few of his shirt buttons. Athletic chic, Rachel thought, if that was even a thing.

She could've sworn Gabe blushed, but he turned toward the end of the hall before she got a good look at him. "Come on," he said. "The field's this way."

Gabe's excitement was palpable as they walked briskly down the hall. But when they approached the entrance to the field from one of the tunnels, Gabe paused, looking up at the empty stands that were illuminated with some of the stadium lights. "I haven't been out here since the team honored me during that last game. It feels strange. Like if I step out on that field, I should be playing."

Rachel looked up at him. She could see the uncertainty in his eyes, feel the sadness in them. It was bittersweet. "Then let's play," she said.

And with that, Gabe's mood seemed to lighten. He put an arm around her and pulled her close, giving her a warm squeeze. "Seriously? I only brought a blanket, figuring we could sit in field and drink the other bottle of wine."

"Seriously," she said. "I'm sure you can find some equipment around here somewhere."

Gabe's small smile seemed to grow as he stared at her until she thought it couldn't possibly get any wider. He looked like a kid whose turn was next to see Santa. "'Kay. I'll be back in a minute." Then he set the wine down and practically bounded down the hall.

A few minutes later, he returned with a bag slung over his shoulder. "Okay, now we might get arrested. I'm not sure whose this is."

Rachel laughed softly. "Guess it's ours now." Then he took her hand in his and stepped out onto the field with Rachel beside him.

"You any good?" he asked once he'd given Rachel a glove and taken one out of the bag for himself. He turned the ball over inside the leather as he waited for her response.

Shrugging, she said, "I'm sure the great Gabriel Torres could teach me a thing or two."

"I'm not sure I'm that great anymore," he replied, and Rachel noticed his expression sober.

Taking his face in her hands, she looked into his dark eyes, which looked lost in thought. "Yeah," she said before giving him a gentle kiss, "you're pretty great. And I'm not just talking about baseball."

When the two broke apart, Gabe smiled and tossed her the ball, which she caught easily since it was underhand and from a few feet away. Then he jogged about ten yards away from her, his bad knee giving out a bit on every step. When he turned back to her, he said, "Okay, now throw it to me."

Rachel hadn't thrown a baseball in years. She'd played softball through her sophomore year of high school, but that had been over a decade ago. Her throw was far enough to make it to Gabe, but her aim was off. Gabe jumped to the side to catch it and winced when he landed. "Sorry," she yelled.

"It's fine," he said before tossing it back. Rachel caught it easily since she didn't even need to move to catch it. "Though it's probably a good idea to play and *then* drink the wine."

"Shut up," she called back with a laugh. But she had to agree with him.

Her aim got better after a few throws, and she was enjoying herself. Over the course of the next half hour or so, Gabe gave her some tips on fielding the ball and taught her how to hit. Since she liked the feel of Gabe behind her as he helped her perfect her swing, she pretended to be even worse than she was.

Not only did she like playing a game she hadn't played since she was a kid, she also took comfort in Gabe's easy demeanor, in the way he seemed to let himself go, like the sport not only had an effect on his body but also on his mind. By the time they settled down on the blanket and opened the wine, his face was almost expressionless. It was as if the game had freed him of any thoughts that had been weighing him down since he left it.

And Rachel had to admit she felt free, too.

CHAPTER SIXTEEN

RACHEL

Over the course of the next week, Rachel made it her mission to discover something about the club that would prove Gabe wasn't involved. At least not to the extent that he had any real ties to it other than possibly being a member. Because when she eventually published the article—she'd have to if the club existed, which she was pretty sure it did—she couldn't let Gabe's name appear in it.

But why would Gabe be receiving statements from Helping Hands if he didn't have direct ties to the club? She hoped that everyone who belonged to the club got a statement like that, but she had no way of knowing. Well, no *ethical* way. It wouldn't make sense that Mike would have chosen Gabe, who had only played in the area for a few years, when Mike most likely had lifelong friends who would be willing and able to inherit the club.

But that revelation did nothing to calm her nerves. Once the story published, her relationship with Gabe would be over. There was no coming back from what she'd done, and she knew that. She couldn't say she was there writing an article about Gabe and then publish one about a secret club, even if

Gabe's name was never linked to it. She'd betrayed his trust. Trust that she valued.

And the truth was, she hadn't found anything worth investigating. At least not without using illegal means to do so. Jared had already gotten some information about the bank, but it had been general information about its location and use. She'd scoured every detail of the customer list he'd sent, but a list of names and addresses didn't mean much. So those people belonged to the bank in some way? That didn't prove anything. There were athletes and non-athletes alike, and she had no way of knowing which ones, if any, were involved in the club.

But then there had been a second email Jared had sent— she assumed with Gabe's financial records—the one she'd seen appear in her inbox but had never opened. Whether her reluctance to take that step was due to her morals or the fact that she was scared she'd see Gabe's role in all of this, she didn't know. Still, the email had remained closed. Though when she'd received it, there was something inside her that told her not to delete it entirely.

She opened her computer and hovered the mouse over Jared's email, which he'd appropriately titled "In case you need it…." She needed it. She *really* needed it. But she couldn't bring herself to look at it. At least not yet.

Picking up her phone, she scrolled through her contacts until she found Rick's name. She hadn't spoken to her boss in a couple weeks, and she knew he'd want good news. Unfortunately, she didn't have any to give him.

When he answered, he sounded hopeful. "Rach, what's new on the Philly beat? You find what you're looking for yet?"

"No one says 'Philly beat,'" Rachel said on a soft laugh, but she was thankful for the short reprieve from her worry.

"And not much, really. That's actually what I called about. I'm kind of stuck. I don't doubt the club exists, but I'm not sure I can prove it. And I have no idea how to find out who the major players are. Has anyone talked to Barnes again? I think he's our best option right now." Rachel could hear how quickly she was talking, but she needed to rip the Band-Aid off and tell Rick she didn't have anything.

She heard Rick sigh heavily. "Barnes is back in rehab. He's not gonna be talkin' to anyone for a while. I already tried, but it's one of those fancy-shmancy places that rich people go to."

It was Rachel's turn to sigh. "I don't know where to go from here, then." She hoped Rick would offer a suggestion or at least a bit of empathy. But she should've known better. Rick was a good guy—and she'd consider him more of a friend than most people would consider their boss—but when it came down to it, Rick had a job to do. And that job involved making sure Rachel did hers.

"Well, you better figure it out quick," Rick snapped. "This may have just been a unicorn in the beginning, but now we *need* it. It's not just your ass on the line, it's mine too. I fought for you to stay in Philly. You think Beckett wanted to spend a small fortune putting you up in some apartment in another city indefinitely?"

She knew Mark Beckett, the magazine's owner, had approved the funding for her investigation, but she didn't know Rick had "fought" for it. She didn't like owing people favors. "I didn't ask you to fight for me."

"No, but that doesn't change the fact that I did. And I did it because I believed you could uncover this story. I believed in *you*. But if Beckett thinks he spent a shit ton of money on something that doesn't pan out, in my mind only one of two things can happen. Beckett'll fire both of us, or he'll only fire you and send somebody to finish what you started down there. You might wanna note that both scenarios involve your sudden unemployment. So before you throw in the towel, you should probably make sure you've exhausted all your options."

"'Kay," was all Rachel could say without her voice shaking audibly. And with that, she said a quick goodbye, told Rick she'd be in touch, and hung up the phone.

GABE

"What's in this thing, a dead body?" Jace leaned down to set the huge box back down on the skid. They'd picked it up only moments earlier before realizing that the two of them probably couldn't move it on their own.

"It's a new blackjack table. Solid oak, so yeah," Gabe said, "it's heavy. That's another downside to owning this place. Can't have anyone deliver anything inside. It was risky enough to have them drop it out front like this." Gabe began pulling the box apart while he spoke. "We gotta put it together anyway, so we can take it inside piece by piece since that'll be easier."

"I charge extra for assembly," Jace joked. "I was hired solely on the assumption that I'd be the muscle."

Gabe stared at him. "You're never the muscle. Speaking of which, I gotta get a new bouncer. One of the guys is moving out to Washington because his daughter's having a baby, and he wants to be closer to it."

Jace shook his head. "It's a human being. You can't just call it an it."

"*You* just did."

Jace looked confused until finally it seemed he realized what Gabe meant.

"And what's with the sudden urge to defend babies? Aly's not pregnant, is she?" The guys pulled most of the box apart and began grabbing some of the pieces to take inside.

"Nah," Jace answered. "But we'll probably try right after we get married. We both want a big family."

"Really?"

"Yeah. Wouldn't it be awesome to have a bunch of little Bennings running around? It'd be like my own personal football team."

Gabe stopped walking and turned around, wondering if he was serious. Why the hell anyone would want a bunch of kids he'd never understand. "I don't know, man. That's a lot of responsibility. And a football team? That's a lot of fuckin' kids. They poop and cry and hit each other, and they want dinner every night." Gabe couldn't even imagine what it was like to have a large family. Growing up, it had only been him and his mom until he moved to the United States. He was used to flying solo, and he'd come to accept it would probably always be that way. At least he was until Rachel had come back into his life.

"I realize what they do, Gabe. I have like a million nieces and nephews," he reminded him before continuing to walk.

"Yeah, but they're not *your* kids. It's different when they're your own, ya know?"

"I guess, yeah. But what do you know about kids?"

Gabe laughed as if the question were ridiculous. "I know more than you think. Running this business is like raising a bunch of children. I have to keep track of what they're doing and who they're talking to, sometimes they ask for more money or complain to me about their coworkers. The struggle is real."

Gabe tried to make his voice light, but he wasn't actually kidding. Running the club had been a lot more difficult than he'd anticipated, and so far the rewards hadn't made up for it. Though he hoped with time they would.

"It can't be *that* bad," Jace said. "The place seems to run smoothly, and the guys seem happy. You'd never know it's been tough on you."

Gabe put a piece of the table down and leaned it carefully against the building so he could open the door, and then Jace held it open while Gabe picked the wood back up again. "That's good to hear," Gabe said. "I guess it's nothing major. That Barnes guy hasn't been bothering me anymore. I don't know." He sighed. "It's all the little shit that adds up to being a pain in the ass. Like the bouncer thing. Oh, and I didn't even tell you that my bank called and said their whole system was hacked a few weeks ago, did I?"

"No. Shit, really?"

"Yeah, it fuckin' sucks. And I don't even know how the bank is handling it or if they have any precautions in place to keep it from happening again. I mean, I'd assume they would up their security, but I have no idea how any of that computer shit works. I can barely order a pizza online."

"Yeah, I hear ya," Jace said as he put down the pieces of the table he'd brought in. "I don't understand much about technology either. I wonder what they could even do with whatever information they got. You don't have a credit card or anything from that bank, do you?"

"No. Nothing. Only the accounts that Mike had set up years ago. The lawyers just had my information transferred onto everything. I let them handle all that and signed whatever papers I was supposed to sign, and that was it. The whole thing makes me nervous, but I don't even know what there is to be nervous about." He ran his hands roughly through his hair in frustration and settled them on the top of his head, sighing deeply. "God, I have no idea what I'm doing."

Jace laughed. "Do you ever?"

CHAPTER SEVENTEEN

RACHEL

When Rachel arrived at the local college stadium, it surprised her how many people were at the baseball camp. When Gabe had told her about the camp he helped with, she had pictured him and a few other guys and a handful of kids from the community. But as she made her way through the venue, which had been set up with various stations where kids could learn different baseball skills, she had a feeling that Gabe had downplayed the camp.

There had to be almost a hundred kids ranging in age from four up to ten—Gabe had said that the following week was the camp for the older age group—and though the camp appeared to have enough staff to successfully run without the supervision of parents, many had chosen to stay in a roped-off section behind one of the dugouts. Rachel had a feeling that had more to do with their desire to perhaps meet the baseball players than it did their desire to see their children improve their skills. The fathers looked starstruck as they looked out over the field intently. And though the moms looked just as pleased to be there, Rachel knew it was probably for a much different reason.

And she couldn't blame them. Seeing so many good-looking guys in tight pants would've made her take a few days off from work too. But since this *was* her job, she didn't have to worry about that. She took her time walking through the camp, getting a few pictures of the players interacting with the children. As she roamed around, she found herself as interested in what was happening around her as the families seemed to.

After about ten minutes, Rachel found Gabe on the other side of the field. He was giving a mini-lesson on fielding to about ten kids who looked to be no older than seven. It reminded her why she never went into a discipline that required her to work with young children: though they were cute, they were nearly impossible to keep focused. Since they didn't typically like to share with one another, they all wanted the ball at the same time, even though it was only Gabe and one other player hitting the ball so they could take turns fielding it.

Gabe saw her and gave her a wave before hitting a grounder to a little boy with dark floppy hair and a few missing front teeth. The boy ran toward it and lowered his glove, but the ball rolled right through his legs. The boy bent over to make a play for the ball, but it was too far under him, so he completely tipped over when he tried to grab it under his legs. A blond girl, who looked slightly older than the boy who'd just missed the play, ran from a few yards away and made the play, causing the boy to burst into tears instantly when he saw the girl had "stolen" his ball. Then he sat down in the grass and pulled his knees to his chest in frustration.

The girl threw the ball back to Gabe, who encouraged the boy to get up and try again. "That happened because there was space between your glove and the grass, Dylan. Make sure your glove touches the ground this time," Gabe called to him. "And don't run up on the ball. Let it come to you." Dylan stared at him but made no move to stand. Gabe immediately jogged out to the boy. He crouched down next to him and put a hand on his shoulder. Gabe said a few words to him, though Rachel couldn't hear what they were, and then put his hand out for Dylan to slap. Gabe turned toward the direction from which he'd come and got into position again. He hadn't waited to see if the boy would stand, but by the time Gabe was ready to hit it again, Dylan was ready to field. Gabe hit a ball right to him this time, and thankfully the boy stopped it. Though it did take him a few tries to pick it up with his glove.

Gabe and the other player continued to hit grounders—and some pop-ups—to the kids, who all seemed like they were having a great time. But what was more fun than watching the children learn about the game was watching Gabe play it with them. From his beaming smile, Rachel could tell he genuinely enjoyed his time there. Despite Gabe having told her when they were at dinner once that he wasn't good with kids, the opposite seemed to be true. That's when she realized that she really didn't have much information about the camp. Other than telling her that he participated in it, Gabe hadn't said much. She didn't know how long he'd been doing it, who was in charge of it, or how the kids participating were chosen. All she knew was that the camp lasted one week per age group and—judging by the way they were dressed—they all got lime green T-shirts when they arrived.

Rachel removed her tablet from her bag and began taking notes and some pictures, though she was careful not to get any of the kids' faces in the shots. She walked over to the parents and assured them that no pictures of their children would be published without their written consent.

Finally there was a break in the action, and Gabe jogged over to her, wrapping his strong arms around her. She had the urge to grab his ass in his tight pants but managed to control herself. She didn't think groping one of the players was appropriate for the setting they were in. That would have to wait until later when they were alone after the dinner they had planned.

"How long have you been here?" Gabe asked. "Did you see Manny? He's around here somewhere." He craned his neck to see over the crowd. He seemed so excited to share the experience with Rachel, and it made her even happier that she'd decided to come.

"Only about twenty minutes," she said, answering his first question. And then, "And no, I didn't see Manny yet. This place is insane. I can't believe what a huge event this is."

"Go big or go home," Gabe said.

"Did you just make that up?" Rachel teased. "That's a clever saying."

"Shut up," he joked. "But seriously, it has gotten pretty big over the years. When we first started it seven years ago, we had like four guys and a few groups of kids. It's really expanded, especially the past few years. More and more guys wanna help, and more kids wanna come. It's pretty awesome."

"Wait," Rachel said, confused. "So you were one of the ones who started this thing?"

"Yeah," Gabe said, looking surprised that she asked him the question. "Didn't I tell you that?"

"No, you didn't tell me that." Rachel's voice grew louder, but it wasn't out of anger. It was out of shock.

"Oh." Gabe shrugged. And the smile on his face let her

know that he knew he'd intentionally left that detail out. "I started it," he said simply. "Well, me and my buddy, Justin. We both got picked up the same year, and we wanted to do something for the community since we were both new to it. Justin's from Atlanta, and he wouldn't have done a thing with his life if it weren't for baseball, so we have that in common."

"You would've done something," Rachel tried to assure him.

"Nope. Probably not," Gabe said casually. "The only reason my mom sent me to this country is because she figured if I had a shot to play baseball in college, I should get a better education than the one I was getting in Puerto Rico. No baseball, no education," he said. "It's that simple."

The next group of kids arrived at Gabe's spot on the field, and the other player instructing the group looked like he was waiting for Gabe to come over so they could begin. "Okay," Gabe said, "I gotta get back to the kids, but if you wanna go talk to Justin, he's over there." Gabe pointed to one of the stations about ten yards away. "He's the one wearing number twelve."

Rachel looked in the direction Gabe had pointed. "Justin Adams?" she asked, though she already knew it was. The Premiers pitcher had two no-hitters and a perfect game on his résumé. But instead of slowing down as he entered his thirties, it seemed he was just getting started. The last two years had been his best seasons by far, but his baseball stats weren't the only thing that came to mind when Rachel thought of Justin. His name had also been on the customer list that Jared had sent her.

The first time she'd gone through all the names, she hadn't even noticed Justin. It might have been because he had such a common name, and there were over fifteen hundred names on the list. But when she'd revisited the document the other day after talking to Rick, she'd noticed Justin because she'd narrowed down the list of people to those in a hundred-mile radius of Philadelphia. Maybe he was her guy.

"Thanks," Rachel said. "I'll go over there for a little bit and talk to him if he has a few minutes free."

Gabe gave her a kiss on the cheek and told her he'd see her later. Then he jogged back over to greet the new group of waiting kids.

Rachel walked around again for a half hour or so, watching the players and kids working on various skills, and then she headed to where Justin was finishing up with a few boys who looked to be nine or ten. He was showing them the proper way to hold a ball and the right way to bring their leg up before a pitch. She waited for the boys to leave before approaching him. It was the first time she introduced herself as Gabriel Torres's girlfriend, though she also identified herself as a reporter doing a story on the retired shortstop.

Justin was more than friendly and answered everything she asked. Unfortunately, she couldn't directly ask him if the club existed—*and oh, by the way, if it does, are you the owner of it?* So she stuck to more innocent topics, like how the camp began and if they do any other volunteer work together. The only bit of information that was pertinent was that he and Gabe couldn't find the time to add anything else major to their plate. Justin had spring training and then the season, so he only had a few months off. And Gabe had his hands full too, though Justin didn't mention with what.

Neither of these guys even had time to run a club like that. There was no way a baseball player who traveled for half the year could have the responsibility of owning and managing an elite club. And there was no way Gabe could do it either. Though he was retired, he was always busy. She'd seen it herself. And now that she was in the picture, he had even less time. The realization sent a wave of relief undulating through her. And until she felt it, she didn't know how badly she'd needed it.

GABE

"What'd you think?" Gabe asked as he trotted over to Rachel. Though his knee was stiff from the day's activities, he couldn't let it show. He didn't want to look like some old washed-up athlete in front of her. Not when he felt like he could conquer the world right now. It had been his first kids camp since his retirement, and though he was nervous beforehand, the day had turned out better than expected.

"It was so great. *You* were great," she answered excitedly. She smiled proudly as she gave him a kiss that required her to turn his cap backward. He fucking loved it. "I can tell how much you love working with these kids," she added.

"Yeah, it's something I'm good at, so it ends up being awesome because we always get a few kids that come back the next year. Some you remember, and some you don't. But it's nice to hear how much they took away from their time here." Gabe packed up some of the equipment and said goodbye to a few kids who were leaving.

"Can't wear your headphones, I guess," she said.

Gabe was confused for a second until he realized what she was talking about. "Oh yeah." He laughed. "Gotta leave those at home. But truthfully, I love interacting with fans. Especially when they're kids. They radiate excitement that's kind of contagious."

"You never get tired of it, though?" Rachel asked. "Like when you're out in public?"

Gabe thought for a moment. "Who's asking? Rachel the reporter, or Rachel my gorgeous girlfriend?" Gabe would never say anything that could lead the public to believe he was bad-mouthing them. And the truth was, the fans weren't his biggest problem.

Rachel smiled. "Your girlfriend wants to know, but I guess it's the reporter asking."

Gabe nodded and adjusted his hat. "To be honest, the fans don't recognize me much. I don't think they expect to see a former professional athlete out and about. The real concern is the media. They're everywhere, always looking for their next big story."

"Hey," Rachel said, tossing a nearby ball at him. "I thought you liked the media."

Gabe smirked. "Eh, some of them are better than others."

"Any ones in particular that you're fond of?" Rachel asked, moving closer to help him put the last few things in his bag. The way she playfully bit her lip as she waited for him to answer made him want to put his own mouth on them.

"Not really," Gabe joked. "They all kind of suck." Anticipating Rachel's playful shove, he moved back to avoid it and laughed when she missed. "Okay, so there may be one I have feelings for," he admitted. Sliding his arms around her waist, he pulled her in close and kissed her gently on her forehead.

"That's good," she said. "Because I have some feelings for a certain baseball player too."

"*Ex*-baseball player," Gabe corrected her.

She shook her head slowly as she gazed up at him, and her eyes told him she knew what he was feeling: that he missed the game, and part of him—the part that wasn't injured—regretted retiring. But as much as she could guess what it was like to leave something you've done your entire life, she would never know how it truly felt. Very few people did. Even his two best friends had no idea. It was one of the reasons he liked talking to other retired players at the club: it felt good to know that people understood where he was coming from.

"Nah," Rachel said, rubbing the back of his short hair with her nails. "You're still a baseball player. Even though you're not in the game anymore, the game will always be in you."

Somehow with that one sentence, she made him feel a little bit better about everything. Because even though he'd lost something, he'd gained something even better.

CHAPTER EIGHTEEN

GABE

"I promise I'll make it up to you," Gabe pleaded.

Rachel looked disappointed, and he couldn't blame her. The first day of the camp had gone so well, and Rachel had stuck around the entire day talking to players, kids, and parents. And now, when he was supposed to be taking her out to dinner, he was bailing on her because he'd gotten a phone call that someone had gotten out of hand at the club after he'd had too much to drink.

When one of the bouncers had called a few minutes ago, he didn't give Gabe much more information than that. But Gabe didn't need to know who it was. The rules were the same as when Mike ran the place: You fuck up one time and you're out. Unlike baseball, guys didn't get three strikes. Whoever was currently being held at the club would remain there until Gabe could come over and talk to him himself. And though he was in no rush to deal with whatever mess awaited him, he wanted the guy out of his club as soon as possible. "Tomorrow?"

The look on Rachel's face told him that might not be good.

"Don't tell me you have plans," he said. "Mine'll be better." He'd make sure of it. He wasn't even sure if Rachel believed he had some sort of family emergency, which is what he'd told her because he couldn't think of anything else that would necessitate him leaving suddenly when they already had plans. It had occurred to him after he'd said it that he didn't even have family in the area. And though she maybe thought that, she didn't know it for sure.

"Okay, I won't tell you I have plans."

Gabe visibly deflated. "Okay, let me go deal with this, and then I'll meet you for a late dinner. I don't need a shower first."

Her expression told him otherwise.

"Fine, maybe I do need a shower."

"I have some work to do tomorrow, but I'll try to take care of everything earlier in the day so we can meet up tomorrow night."

"Really?" Gabe breathed a sigh of relief and smiled warmly at her. "Thank you. I promise... Anything you wanna do, we'll do. You name it."

"Okay, there's that new sushi place on Front Street I've been wanting to try."

"I meant *almost* anything," he said. "You know I don't eat sushi."

The smile she gave him let him know that the dinner menu was her little punishment for bailing on her tonight. "You will tomorrow," she said.

He couldn't help but smile back.

RACHEL

Rachel had spent most of the next morning researching the

Bank of American Fidelity's customers who resided in the Philadelphia area, convinced there had to be one who would talk to her and give her some tiny nugget of information that would allow her to uncover the club in a way that wouldn't make Gabe hate her.

Then she quickly realized that was wishful thinking.

Of all the people in the area, there were only twenty-seven who weren't current athletes, and that included Gabe. And of those, only fourteen had never played a professional sport. She guessed that those were most likely club employees, especially since some of the names were women.

After a little digging around on social media, Rachel was able to narrow down the list to two possible women who might be willing to talk to her for a price. The first was Rebecca. She was a beautiful, single bartender who currently worked part-time at a local restaurant. And from the posts on her page, Rachel learned she had aspirations of becoming a model. Though as far as Rachel could tell that dream hadn't panned out yet. But if Rebecca worked at the club at one point, she might still. From her Facebook, Rachel didn't see any evidence of a current full-time job, and speaking with her wasn't a risk Rachel was willing to take if Rebecca was a current employee.

That left her with Jamie, a divorced mother of two who, from the looks of her page, had a few part-time jobs waiting tables around the city. Like Rebecca, she was beautiful. A few of her older posts mentioned not having much money around the holidays, and from the looks of her pictures, she appeared to live in a small apartment. Rachel hoped that meant that Jamie was no longer employed by the club because she figured an elite establishment such as that would pay its employees better than whatever Jamie seemed to be bringing home currently.

Left without any other options, Rachel chose to pursue the only lead she had. She entered the small diner right after the lunch rush and took a look around, hoping like hell Jamie would be there. Finally, luck seemed to be on her side, and she approached the counter where Jamie was working alone. There were only two other customers still seated, and Rachel chose a stool toward the end so she was as far away as she could get from them.

"I'll be right with you," Jamie said as she set down a burger and fries for someone.

Rachel said thank you and took a menu from between the napkin and sugar dispensers. A minute or so later, after Jamie had rung someone up, she found her way over to Rachel. "What can I get for ya?" Now that Jamie was closer to her, Rachel could tell she was older than she looked in her pictures online. The wrinkles around the corners of her eyes told Rachel the woman was probably in her forties, and the dark circles below them meant she probably didn't get much sleep.

"Iced tea to start. Not sure what I want to eat yet. You have any suggestions?" Rachel asked.

"You ever been here before?"

"Nope, just moved to the city not that long ago."

"Well, welcome to the City of Brotherly Love," Jamie said. She gave Rachel what appeared to be a genuine smile, but it wasn't as full as it could've been. "I'd go with the gyro and, if you have time for dessert, a cinnamon bun. People love 'em."

Rachel smiled. "Sounds good. I'll trust you."

Jamie wrote down the order and said she'd be back in a moment with her drink. When she returned, Rachel asked her about the bracelet she was wearing. "Is that sand inside?" Rachel asked, looking at the thin clear plastic tube around the woman's wrist.

"Yeah, my daughter gave it to me."

Rachel liked that Jamie didn't seem embarrassed by wearing something a child made. It made her endearing in a way Rachel hadn't expected. "That's sweet. How old is she?" From the pictures online, Jamie's little girl looked to be about six.

"She's seven, but she made this when she was in preschool. Me and my ex split custody, so I like to wear something from the kids the weeks he has them." She pulled at a thin chain around her neck that had been tucked into her white shirt. "From my son. He's eleven." Then she shook her head and began wiping the counter again even though she just had. "I have no idea why I'm telling you all this. You must think I'm crazy," she said. "Who tells some stranger she just met about her life?"

Rachel shrugged. "I'm used to it. I'm a reporter. I hear all kinds of things."

"What'da you write for the paper or something?"

"A sports magazine. It's actually why I'm here," Rachel admitted.

"In Philly?"

Rachel swallowed her iced tea. "In this diner, actually."

Jamie stopped cleaning and looked up at her curiously.

"I had a couple of questions for you if you have the time to answer them."

Looking guarded and skeptical, Jamie crossed her arms in front of her chest. "You have questions for *me*? What's this about?"

Rachel looked around to see if the one customer still remaining was paying attention, but thankfully he was on his phone. "I'm guessing you know the answer to that,"

"I don't. And if you're not gonna tell me, this conversation's over. I actually think it's over anyway."

Sighing, Rachel thought carefully about what to say. "It's about Mike Tarino. I think you used to work for him."

"I don't know who that is," Jamie said simply, but the way she averted her eyes and played with her fingernails told Rachel that Jamie knew exactly who Mike was.

"Is fifteen hundred enough?"

"What?" Jamie narrowed her eyes.

"Fifteen hundred dollars. To answer a few questions about when you worked for Tarino. Truthfully, of course," Rachel added.

Jamie scoffed. "So I worked for a guy I don't even know? Doing what exactly?"

Rachel knew Jamie was testing her to find out what she already knew, and she couldn't blame her. Though the money was probably tempting, Jamie's fear of what might happen if she talked probably overshadowed it. "You worked at his club, right?"

Jamie pursed her lips but didn't respond.

"For high-profile athletes," Rachel said. "I already know it exists. I just need to know who's running it."

Jamie picked at some crumbs on her black apron before putting her hands into its pockets. "If a place like that existed," Jamie said, her voice hushed, "anyone who worked there would've probably signed an NDA to make sure they didn't talk about it."

Rachel wasn't surprised that Jamie brought up a nondisclosure agreement. She was prepared for Jamie to. "Well, Mike Tarino's been dead for months. I doubt a dead guy will sue for violating such an agreement." She stared into

Jamie's eyes empathetically. "Look, you could use the money, and I could use the information. We'd be helping each other out."

Jamie thought for a few moments, shaking her leg nervously. "You won't reveal your source?"

Rachel put her right hand up and shook her head no. "Promise."

A minute or so of silence passed between them, and Rachel knew Jamie was using the time to decide what to do. The fact that she was even considering it was a good sign, so Rachel wouldn't pressure her any more than she already had.

"Two grand," Jamie finally said. "I have bills due next week."

Rachel gave her a quick nod. "Two grand. Fifteen hundred now and I'll come back with the other five. I don't have it with me." Rick had only approved fifteen hundred, but Rachel would pay the other five hundred herself.

"Okay," Jamie said. "What is it you want to know?"

Everything. She wanted to know everything. But there was one thing she cared about more than any other. "Who's running the club now?"

"No idea," Jamie replied. "That's the truth. I haven't worked there in two years. That was long before Mike died, obviously."

"Why'd you leave?"

Jamie rubbed her forehead in what seemed to be frustration. "I was going through a divorce, and I needed to give the court financial statements and info about where I worked. I didn't want to risk this all coming out. Mike was... He was a real sweet guy. I didn't want to cause him any trouble. And I wasn't as strapped for cash at that time, either." Jamie looked down and wrung the towel between her hands, looking almost sick as she told Rachel all of this.

Rachel felt awful for putting her in this position, but she'd already started this. She had to finish it. "You weren't worried your husband would tell the courts?"

"He didn't know. I told him it was something I couldn't talk about. As long as the money was coming in, he didn't care where it came from."

The guy sounded like a real winner. But Rachel kept that thought to herself and instead focused on the task at hand. "The money was good then?" Rachel figured it would have been, but she still wanted confirmation, which she got when Jamie nodded. "But you said you don't know who's running the place now?"

"Nope. Once I cut ties with the place, I didn't look back. No one would've told me anything about it anyway."

"Right," Rachel said. "That makes sense." She dropped her head into her hands and let out a frustrated sigh.

When Rachel lifted her head, Jamie was studying her face like there was something she couldn't quite figure out. "Why are you so interested in who's in charge now? You said you already know the place exists. Isn't that the story?"

It was. But Rachel didn't exactly have proof of the club, other than her conversation with Jamie. One anonymous source wouldn't be enough to write a story like this one. "Yeah," she answered. "It is. But I need to know. If for no other reason than to satisfy my own curiosity."

Jamie nodded silently but didn't ask anything further. Whether she believed Rachel or not, Rachel couldn't tell. "I'm surprised you didn't ask how Mike recruited people."

"Recruited people?"

"Yeah. Members, employees … There's no way to join a place that doesn't exist, right?" she asked.

The corner of Rachel's mouth turned up in excitement as she sat up straighter. "How did Mike recruit people?" she asked, her eyes never leaving Jamie's.

"Business cards," she said. "If I wanted to know who was head of the place now, I'd go to a high-profile sporting event and see who's handing them out." And with that, Jamie walked away from her to brew a new pot of coffee. "Leave the money on the counter before you go," she said simply.

And that's exactly what Rachel did.

CHAPTER NINETEEN

GABE

"Everything go okay last night?" Rachel asked as Gabe got back into his car.

He was thankful she hadn't followed through on her threat to make him eat sushi and had instead agreed to Chinese takeout, which he'd grabbed after picking her up. She said she was tired from the day and didn't feel like getting dressed up anyway. Gabe could relate. Last night hadn't been the most relaxing.

"Yeah," he answered. "It's all good now." Gabe neglected to tell her that "it" was some piece of shit basketball player who thought Gabe's club was an appropriate place to grope one of the cocktail waitresses. He suspected that it was the same guy who had caused the one bartender to quit, but he had no way of knowing for sure. Gabe had told him in no uncertain terms that he was never to come back to the establishment and if he spoke of the situation or the club to anyone else, he'd regret it.

Short of suing the twentysomething, there wasn't much Gabe could do if the guy didn't make good on his promise. It wasn't like Gabe was running some sort of nineteen twenties Scottish mafia where he would cut this guy's cheeks if he talked. Still, Gabe figured a vague threat might be enough to make the guy wonder what Gabe and his guys were capable of. "What about you? You get everything done you needed to do?"

Gabe looked to Rachel, who was staring out the window at the rain as he drove the few blocks back to his place.

"I did. Just work stuff. I was out a lot of the day."

"Oh yeah? Anything interesting?" He figured it had to do with the article she was writing on him, and he wondered what she'd been up to. When she didn't respond right away, he joked, "You were spying on me, weren't you?"

Rachel seemed to startle at his words and then assured him she'd never do that.

"Sure, sure," he teased. "Thought maybe you were peeping in my windows from the roof across the street or something."

When she turned toward him, resting her head on her hand as she propped her elbow on the car door, he noticed the small smile playing on her lips. "If I were going to peep in your windows, I'd get a better vantage point than *that*," she said.

"Oh yeah? Like where? It sounds like you've given this some thought."

Rachel shrugged. "Like your bedroom."

Gabe raised an eyebrow. "You're welcome in my bedroom anytime," he said, placing a hand on her thigh after turning into his parking garage.

"Oh yeah?"

"Yup. The door's always open." He felt her relax with his touch, the muscles in her leg loosening. When he parked the car, he looked over at her, taking in the way her deep green eyes seemed to sparkle in the dim light of the parking garage. He could feel the pull between them, like there was a force drawing them to one another that they couldn't fight even if they tried. Not that he'd want to. Every moment with Rachel made him wonder how he'd gone so many years without her.

"How do you feel about cold Chinese food?" she asked before leaning in the rest of the way to kiss him softly. Her mouth opened for him instantly, her lips soft and wet.

Gabe felt himself harden, and he adjusted his jeans to accommodate the bulge that now filled them. He didn't know if he'd even be able to wait until they got inside the building to start undressing her, much less inside his apartment. The way her body responded to even the softest touch had him wanting to climb over the console and take her right there in his car.

Truthfully, there was nothing to stop him. His parking space was relatively private, near the corner of the garage with a concrete pillar obscuring them from view. He realized rather quickly that if she was game, *he* certainly was. Sliding a hand under Rachel's shirt, it wasn't long before Gabe had her almost completely naked from the waist up. And though he'd waited for a signal that she didn't want to do this here, she hadn't given him one.

Instead, her hips lifted off the seat, giving him easier access to the button on her jeans, which were so tight he wasn't sure he could remove them in the confined space. "I've never had this problem," he said, yanking her pants down as gently as he could. "But I can't get these off."

The comment caused Rachel to laugh out loud. Then she wiggled beneath his hand as she helped him slide them down. Before she could take them off completely, she kicked off her boots. "You have too many clothes on," she said, already lifting his shirt to pull over his head.

Once the article of clothing was off, Rachel's fingers were on Gabe's abs as they traced along the lines between them. His muscles flexed at the cool touch of her skin against his, and he could already feel how ready he was. He wanted to grab himself, dull the ache that was throbbing inside his pants, but Rachel's hand got there first.

As soon as she made contact with his cock, rubbing him through his jeans, he knew he wouldn't last as long as he wanted to. It was hard and fast and fucking frantic, like she couldn't get enough of him. "Jesus," he said, and he could hear how harsh and unsteady his voice sounded. With a sudden gasp, Gabe found himself putting his hand on hers to stop her movement. "No more."

Though she paused for a moment to unzip his pants, springing his erection free in the process, she went right back to touching him. But this time it was with her mouth. He willed himself to think of anything else but Rachel's mouth on his cock, but the effort was in vain. As her lips wrapped around him, warmth spread through his body, and soon enough he was thrusting into her mouth wildly. His hands tangled with her hair as it fell over his lap, and he thought how easily he could come from watching her. "Christ, Rach. This is so fucking good."

He thought he felt her smile, but she went right back to sucking him. And as her wet lips slipped slowly over him, his hips began to buck frantically. "Rachel, I'm going to... God, you have to..." He couldn't even get out the last word of warning before he was coming. And though he'd tried to pull away, Rachel's lips stayed tightly locked around him, licking every drop of his release as it shot into her mouth.

"That was incredible," he said once she pulled away from him and he was able to get his brain working again. He didn't miss the way she licked her lips as she looked into his eyes. It was one of the sexiest things he'd ever seen. "Now I think it's your turn."

RACHEL

A few moments later, Rachel was lying on the black leather of Gabe's back seat, the lower half of her body in the air as Gabe's face nestled between her legs. His movements were slow and calculated as he licked and sucked on all her sensitive areas. She couldn't even remember the last time someone had done this to her. Somehow, it was so much more intimate than sex, more vulnerable. But with Gabe, Rachel found herself able to open up to him, expose parts of herself inside and out that she'd never felt comfortable sharing with anyone before.

Rachel's legs draped over Gabe's shoulders, but she could already feel them growing weak. Making him come had turned her on almost as much as what he was currently doing, and she knew she wouldn't last long, especially now that he was picking up the pace. The sounds that escaped from her were barely recognizable, even to her. She was a mess of gasps and moans, sharp inhalations and shuddering sighs as she struggled to hold off the release she knew was close. She didn't even care that she could hear how wet she was with every stroke of Gabe's tongue. The fact that he seemed to be enjoying himself only turned her on more. She was needy and frantic and on the edge of an orgasm she knew would be one of the most amazing she'd had in recent memory.

But she didn't want to give in to it because letting go would mean an end to . . . this. And *this*, as far as she was concerned, was as close to heaven as someone on earth could get. Gabe let go of one of her thighs to put a hand on her breast. Her skin lit up at his touch, and when his fingers focused their attention on her nipple, she lost it completely. Waves of pleasure shot through her as her body tried to clench around Gabe's tongue. It was so warm, so smooth, in such contrast to how his cock felt when he was inside her. But it was no less pleasurable. This, right here, was perfect.

Slowly, Gabe lowered her back down, kissing all the way up her torso until his lips reached her neck. They lay there together for a few minutes, cocooned in a perfect bubble of sated bliss. But like all good things, it eventually had to come to an end.

They put their clothes back on in satisfied silence, every so often exchanging glances that spoke more than words could've. Once inside Gabe's apartment, they heated their food and settled down on the couch to watch a movie. "I totally forgot to ask you," Gabe said after swallowing a bite of his orange chicken. "There's a party after the first night of the draft that I'm going to. I was hoping I wouldn't have to go alone." He raised an eyebrow at her curiously.

Rachel couldn't resist. "Who are you thinking of asking?"

For a second, Gabe looked confused, but then his expression relaxed into a smile. "You're messing with me, aren't you?"

Rachel let out the laugh she'd been holding in. "Yeah," she said. "I'm surprised you fell for it. I'd be happy to go."

"Good. It's a date then."

"It's a date," she confirmed. "Now tell me about the party." As much as she wanted to go with Gabe because he was her boyfriend, the reporter in her couldn't ignore the fact that the event had fallen into her lap. Since her conversation with Jamie, Rachel had been wondering where she might be able to see someone handing out cards for the club.

Gabe told her the party was being held at the football stadium in one of the spaces that was used for weddings and other fancy events. It was obviously invite only and would have newly drafted players as well as established professional athletes. If there were ever an event where Rachel had a chance of finding out who was running the club, this was it.

"Sounds great," Rachel said. "I'm looking forward to it."

CHAPTER TWENTY

RACHEL

Rachel loved dressing up. It reminded her of pretending to be a princess when she was a little girl. And even though she was going in at least a partially professional capacity, she was also excited to get to wear a beautiful dress. Her emerald silk gown with an organza overlay on the bodice wrapped around one shoulder and fell smoothly to the floor. She'd put her hair into a French braid that wrapped around one side of her head before being pinned up into a bun. As she looked in the mirror, she thought she looked good. She hoped Gabe would think so as well.

He was due to pick her up any second, so she spread some tinted gloss on her lips, grabbed her silver clutch, and went into the living room to wait. His timing was impeccable because she heard a knock at the door as soon as she made it through the short hall.

Smoothing her hands down her dress, she took a deep breath before opening the door. Her jaw dropped as she took in the sight of Gabe in a tailored, dark-gray suit. Underneath, he wore a crisp navy shirt that he left open at the collar so a hint of his bronze skin showed. He was seriously smoking hot.

"Wow," was all she could say.

"Wow to you too," he said with that sexy smile that always made her clit throb. He leaned in to give her a kiss on the cheek and then whispered in her ear, "I can't wait to peel that off you."

Even more heat rushed south as his words sent a shiver through her. "Maybe we should do that now," she said, her voice husky.

But Gabe, the bastard, pulled back and shoved his hands in his pockets, which made his suit jacket rise and his pants tighten across the front of him. "Good things come to those who wait."

"I'm perfectly able to come without waiting."

Gabe barked out a laugh. "I have no doubts about that. But still, I have a car downstairs, and I'm looking forward to showing you off to everyone."

His comment was classic, sweet Gabe, and there was no way she could refuse it. "Let's go then." She acted put out, but she was excited to go.

The car ride was relatively quick since the party was being held on one of the upper floors of the football stadium, which was close to where Gabe lived. She was amazed that they could fit such a large, glamorous space inside of a stadium, but there it was—all crystal chandeliers and linen-covered tables. They found Jace quickly, and Rachel was introduced to his fiancée, Alessandra, who was sweet in a slightly awkward way that Rachel found thoroughly endearing. The four of them mingled, with Gabe and Jace introducing the women to countless people—many of whom Rachel either knew or at least knew of. Alessandra looked uncomfortable though.

"You okay?" Rachel whispered to her as they stood at a high-top table and the guys talked to a few other men about the new turf the stadium had put down.

Alessandra jolted a little at the sound of Rachel's voice, but smiled shyly. "Yes, I'm fine. I'm just not much of a people person." She chuckled in a self-deprecating way that made Rachel like the beautiful doctor even more.

"Honestly? Me neither. But I have to fake it for my job," Rachel said. That wasn't entirely true. She did like meeting people, but she also needed a serious recharge afterward. Crowds often overwhelmed her though, and a lot of her calm composure was a facade that she'd perfected over years of attending events like this.

"Yeah, I'm fine if I'm in my own element, but this"— Alessandra gestured around the room—"is decidedly *out* of my element."

"Maybe we'll stumble across a team doctor for you to chat with," Rachel offered with a smile, which Alessandra returned.

"Maybe."

"Want anything to drink?" Gabe asked her.

"Sure. White wine is fine."

"Great. Want anything, Aly?"

"I think we're going to take a walk over to the appetizers," Jace said as he put an arm around Alessandra's waist.

"Fat bastard," Gabe taunted.

Jace patted his flat stomach with his hand. "You know it."

"You want to come with me or wait here?" Gabe asked her after Jace and Alessandra walked away.

"I'll wait here and save our table."

"Okay, I'll be right back."

She watched Gabe walk off before she glanced around the room. Taking in the diverse crowd, she allowed herself to enjoy existing on the fringe for a minute. Rachel was an observer through and through, and people-watching was one of her favorite pastimes.

But when she saw a man surreptitiously hand a recent draftee a card, her entire body tensed. She watched them speak for a moment as the player slipped the card into his pocket and the two men shook hands. Her eyes tracked the movements of the man who'd handed out the card. He was tall and lithe, his black suit hugging his frame. His blond hair was mussed in that intentional way that made it seem as though he'd just been riding in a convertible with the top down. He approached another young athlete and repeated the process all over again.

"Here ya go," Gabe said as he put her drink down in front of her.

Rachel felt like she'd nearly jumped out of her skin, but Gabe hadn't seemed to notice. "Thanks," she said as she lifted the glass to her lips. Gabe stood next to her, his hand on the small of her back and his thumb caressing her over the fabric of her dress as he made small talk. She hated that she wasn't fully in the moment with him. Hated that she couldn't stop her brain from thinking about who the man might have been and how she was going to get close enough to him to figure it out.

Gabe, unbeknownst to him, gave her an opportunity. "Hey, I'm going to run to the restroom. You want me to track down Jace and Aly for you, or are you good here for a few minutes?"

"I'm good." She felt like she'd said the words too abruptly, so she willed herself to calm down before continuing. "I actually might mingle a little. See what stories I can sniff out." She said the words with a smile that she hoped hid the fact that she was serious.

"Sounds good. I'll find you in a few minutes."

"No worries. I'll be fine."

Gabe leaned in and gave her a soft kiss. "I know." With that, he went off in the direction of where she assumed the bathrooms were.

Rachel gave a quick look around. She'd lost sight of the man who'd handed out the cards, so she had little choice but to wander around and hope she stumbled upon him. She walked around, becoming more disappointed as time passed. She figured he must have left already, the dread of the missed opportunity weighing heavily on her. But as soon as she'd had the thought, the man materialized in front of her.

"Excuse me," he said with a gleaming smile as he tried to slide past her.

"No problem." She extended her hand toward him, unwilling to let him get away again. "I'm a reporter with *All Access Sports*."

The man's smile grew in response, and he grasped her hand in a firm shake. "Chad Weller. Nice to meet you."

She nodded. "It's a beautiful event," she said as she looked around the room. "Lots of great athletes." Rachel was desperately trying to think ahead as she spoke, to come up with some way of finding out more about Chad.

"Yeah, it sure is. You came down here for the draft? Isn't *All Access* based out of New York?"

"I'm down here on a story," she answered. "What do you do?" she asked, wanting to steer the conversation back to him.

"I'm an agent."

Her heart sank. "Oh." Forcing a smile, she continued, "Bet you've found plenty of prospective clients tonight."

"Yeah, I've handed out my fair share of cards," he said as he returned her smile. He pulled one out of his pocket and handed it to her. "In case you're ever in need of an agent's services."

She took it, unsure if his comment was genuine or laced with innuendo. Deciding it wasn't worth hanging around to find out, she quickly excused herself and went off to find Gabe.

With every step she took, Rachel did her best to quell the frustration she felt. At least now she could stop obsessing and focus on having a good night with her date. She made her way off in the direction in which Gabe had walked. Her eyes settled on him a minute later, and a smile automatically spread across her lips. Yes, she could definitely enjoy the night with her man.

Except, as she approached, she saw Gabe talking to two football players who played in the very stadium she currently stood in. And Gabe was handing them each a small, black card.

GABE

"We're having an event tomorrow night to celebrate the end of the draft, if you guys are interested."

Patrick Reardon and Lamar Tannis nodded solemnly, letting Gabe know they were taking him seriously.

"And no one is permitted in without an invitation from me. So don't spread word around about where you're going. You follow the rules, and we'll get along just fine." Gabe internally laughed at this persona he had to put on in these instances. It was so unlike him in every facet of his life besides moments like this. He felt like a complete imposter.

"We understand," Lamar said as he held out his hand to shake Gabe's. "We won't say a word."

Gabe shook each man's hand firmly. "Then I look forward to seeing you tomorrow." He gave them each one final nod before he turned around. And came face-to-face with Rachel.

Plastering on a casual smile, he approached her quickly and began ushering her away from Lamar and Patrick. "Hey. Been having fun?"

"Yeah. I've been networking. How about you?"

Gabe slung an arm around her shoulders. "Yup. Just welcoming a few of the new guys to the city."

"They must be excited," she said. She felt a little stiff as they walked. He wondered if her feet were hurting or something.

"Yeah, I think so. A couple of us volunteered to take them out on the town tomorrow night. Show them all that Philly has to offer." The lie came to him out of nowhere, but he was thankful for it. It would give him an out to go to the club the next night without her being suspicious.

"Oh yeah? I bet they were thrilled with that." She looked up at him with a full smile. He wasn't sure if she was teasing him or not, but her smile seemed genuine.

"They seemed into it."

Rachel tucked herself into his side. "Where are you guys going to take them?"

To a club I own and can never tell you anything about. "Not sure yet. We'll probably figure it out as we go."

They chatted more as they did another loop around the room. They met back up with Jace and Aly, and the two couples spent some time on the dance floor. As Gabe held Rachel close while they swayed slowly to the music, the movement quickly became a kind of foreplay.

Gabe trailed his fingers down her spine and sucked on her earlobe. Finally, he whispered, "You about ready to get out of here?"

"I thought you'd never ask," she replied.

Gabe gave her temple a soft kiss before pulling away and grabbing her hand. They said quick goodbyes to Jace and Aly, who also looked ready to spend some time alone together. Then Gabe whisked her out of there, into the car, and back to his place.

They'd barely made it inside before Gabe had her pressed against a wall, trailing kisses down every shred of bare skin. They were naked soon after. As he laid her back on his bed and pressed inside her—and the kittens scurried out from their hiding spot—Gabe knew that he could do this forever. Not just the sex, but all the rest of it too. Going to events, sitting at home watching TV, having a quiet dinner with friends. He could see himself doing all of it for the rest of his life. As long as Rachel was the one he got to do it with.

As they both frantically chased their orgasms, their chests heaving, fingernails grazing across skin, their kisses consuming each of them, he knew that Rachel was right there with him. She would be the last girlfriend he would ever have. Of that, he was sure.

And as they both climaxed, first Rachel and then Gabe seconds later, for the first time in a long time, Gabe felt like he was exactly where he was supposed to be.

CHAPTER TWENTY-ONE

RACHEL

Rachel rested back on the pillow mountain she'd made on Gabe's bed and waited for him to get out of the shower. She stretched out, her gaze sweeping across the room before it locked onto his wallet on the dresser. Biting the side of her cheek, Rachel warred with herself. There was no way Gabe could've stashed away the cards since he'd been otherwise... occupied all evening.

Climbing out of the bed slowly, she made her way toward the dresser and picked up the wallet. It was heavy in her hand as she cast a quick look toward the bathroom before returning her eyes to the soft leather in her palm.

Opening it felt as wrong as opening the email from Jared, but it would also let her know once and for all if Gabe was involved. She had no idea how much time passed as she stood there and contemplated opening the wallet. But it was evidently long enough for Gabe to finish his shower, because she startled at the sound of the door opening. She quickly threw the wallet back on the dresser, causing it to knock over a picture frame of Gabe, Jace, and Ben.

Gabe, who had been drying his hair with a towel, jerked

his head up to look at her. "You okay?" he asked.

"Yeah. Totally. I was just…" She scooped up the picture frame and showed it to Gabe. "Looking at this picture of you guys. You look so young."

Gabe chuckled. "Yeah, we were still in college. You want breakfast?" Gabe asked.

"Um, I guess that depends."

"On what?" He changed into a pair of worn dark jeans and a crisp white V-neck T-shirt and motioned for her to follow him into the kitchen.

"On whether I'll be the one making it."

Gabe chuckled as he ran a hand through his hair and turned to the microwave, stooping a bit so he could see his reflection as he pushed his hair up and over to one side. "What? You don't trust my culinary skills?"

"The opposite. I was kind of hoping you were going to make something. I'm not really in the mood to cook. I guess my domestic capabilities begin and end at cleaning."

"I don't expect you to cook and clean for me, you know?" he said, raising an eyebrow at the suit and dress she'd picked up from the living room floor as they'd walked through it. "This isn't the nineteen fifties."

"Good, because I don't think I could wear a dress every day."

"But you look so hot in them," he said with a pout that was obviously intentional.

Rachel laughed and shook her head like she was bothered by his comment when they both knew it was the opposite.

Gabe took the clothes from her hands after he'd finished fixing his hair and washing his hands. "I actually thought we'd go to this place a few blocks down. A little mom-and-pop joint that makes a killer breakfast. I used to go there all the time, and it would only be locals. But then the place was featured on one of those diner shows, and tourists found out about it. I haven't been there in a while."

"Sure, that sounds great," she agreed. "Let me just get ready."

"No rush," he said. "We can drop these at the cleaners too while we're out."

It occurred to her how routine that sounded: like they'd been together for years and were running out to take care of some weekend errands. "Perfect," she said before heading into the bathroom for a shower.

The fifteen-minute walk from Gabe's to the diner was a welcome one. Though the air was chilly in the early spring morning, it felt refreshing, allowing her to clear her mind for the first time in a long time. Gabe talked about his time in the city and how he'd be happy to make the trip to New York to visit her once she had to go home.

Though his gesture was comforting, it reminded her of something she'd tried so hard to forget recently: her time with Gabe was limited in more ways than one. And the thought wasn't one she wanted to dwell on. She'd enjoy what time she did have left with him. "What's good at this place?" she asked as Gabe opened the door for her to step inside. A bell rung with their entrance, and they were greeted by a young waitress with a tight blond bun and a warm smile who told them to sit anywhere they'd like and she'd be over soon to take their orders.

A minute after they sat down, the server appeared with two menus and took their drink orders.

"To answer your question . . . stuffed French toast," Gabe

said. "It's the best. And not a lot of places have it."

"What's it stuffed with?" Rachel asked, scanning her menu for the item.

"Whatever you want." Gabe pointed to the spot on Rachel's menu that had the choices. "I usually get strawberries and cream cheese, but they have Nutella or peanut butter and bananas. They even make one like a breakfast sandwich with sausage, egg, and cheese inside."

Rachel looked over the choices, thinking how amazing everything sounded: fresh-baked pastries, build-your-own omelets, specialty pancakes. Ultimately, she decided on an omelet with spinach and mushrooms with a side of bacon. When she declined the toast, Gabe asked the waitress to bring it out anyway because he'd eat it.

"Enough carbs?" Rachel joked after the waitress left.

Gabe scoffed as if the question were ludicrous. "No such thing," he said.

Sipping on coffee, they waited for their food. Gabe showed her a trick that involved balancing two forks linked together on a toothpick. It was utterly ridiculous, and Rachel loved every second of it. Just as she started to think how childlike she probably seemed as she tried to do it herself with Gabe's help, a little boy appeared beside their table. The man next to him, who Rachel assumed was his father, had a hand on the kid's shoulder as he spoke. "Sorry to bother you, but me and my son just happened to look over here while we were eating and... You're Gabriel Torres, right?"

"That would be me," Gabe said with a nod. "What can I do for you gentlemen?"

"Um, my son was hoping he could get your autograph. He wanted a picture, but I told him that would be too much. We don't want to interrupt your meal."

It occurred to Rachel that they kind of already were, but of course she'd never say that.

Gabe gave the kid a friendly smile and began to slide out of the booth. "No, it's fine. Really. Our food hasn't even come out yet. I'm happy to do it."

The man seemed more excited than his son, but Rachel kept that comment to herself too. Instead she said, "Would you like to get in the picture, too? I'll be happy to take it." She extended her hand toward the man, who already had his phone out.

The man's face lit up with the offer, and for the first time, Rachel could see what Gabe had been talking about when he'd said that fans weren't the problem. Most of the time they were friendly and appreciative, and in this case, completely starstruck. Gabe had been able to make this guy's day with nothing more than a few kind words and a smile.

Rachel knew how the man felt. Gabe had the same effect on her.

By the time they left the diner, it was almost two hours later. Gabe hadn't been kidding about the place being a popular tourist attraction. What had begun as a quick picture with a father and son escalated rapidly. Once a few people recognized Gabe, others wanted in on the action, practically lining up at Rachel and Gabe's table to get an autograph or a picture with the baseball player. Though the staff at the restaurant did their best to give the two some privacy, Gabe's willingness to appease the crowd only made them more inclined to interact with him. It made Rachel feel conflicted in a way she hadn't before.

As part of the media, she'd never thought much about what it might feel like to be on the opposite side of things. To have questions and comments thrown your way without regard for their potential impact on the person on the receiving end. Gabe fielded questions about his early retirement and the upcoming season of a team he didn't even play for anymore. He was even asked who Rachel was. And somehow, he addressed all the comments with dignity and ease, despite the condescending manner with which some of them were obviously posed.

"That was pretty impressive," Rachel said to him when they were finally able to leave without ignoring anyone.

"What's that?" Gabe asked her, putting an arm on her shoulder as they crossed the street.

"How you handled all that back there. Those people were all over you, and some of them weren't even fans. They wouldn't have even recognized you if other people hadn't."

Gabe smiled, but it looked halfhearted. "The years of practice paid off. I guess, in that way, it's like a sport."

Rachel had never thought about it like that, but the ability to please both the fans and media without giving in to their every request was a talent in and of itself. But before she got the opportunity to tell him that, a strange ring interrupted her thoughts. "What's that?" she asked, looking over to Gabe as he fished his phone from his pocket.

"That," he said with an amused shake of his head, "would be Camille Facetiming me." He turned the phone so she could see Camille's face. It looked like she was outside, but Rachel couldn't tell where.

"You going to answer it?"

"Now?" Gabe seemed surprised that Rachel would suggest that.

"Well, yeah. You can't answer later. She's calling now."

Gabe chuckled. "I know. But I can't be one of those people who breaks their neck walking on a sidewalk because they were too involved in whatever was on their phone to watch what they were doing. And I'm spending time with *you* right now. We were already interrupted during breakfast. I can talk to Camille later. I doubt it's important." Gabe looked down at his phone when it stopped ringing and made a motion to put it back in his pocket. "Guess the decision was made for me," he said, but was cut off by the phone ringing again.

Rachel laughed. "Stop walking and answer it."

Gabe rolled his eyes, but the, "Yes, dear," he gave Camille when he answered had him smiling.

"What are you doing right now?"

"That's a dumb question. I'm talking to you."

Camille ignored his smartass response and dived right in to the reason for her call. "I'm looking for a new car right now, and I need your opinion on it."

"What happened to your car?"

"Some transmission thing. Wasn't even worth fixing when I learned of all the other stuff that was wrong with it."

"Oh shit. Sorry to hear that."

"It's okay. I like to believe that she went to a beautiful place called car heaven where she can drive around in the sun with her other car friends. I'm sure she's up there speeding down an open highway without a cop in sight."

"That's a nice thought," Gabe said. "Molly lived a long, full life and was extremely loved. It was her time."

The comments made Rachel laugh, but they also made

her take notice of how easily the two friends talked, how well they knew each other. Gabe knew the name of Camille's car, and to Rachel's knowledge, Gabe didn't even know if Rachel owned a car. Somehow now that seemed significant to her, even though she knew it wasn't. At least, not really.

It wasn't like knowing if someone had a car or not was the key to compatibility or relationship sustainability. Logically, Rachel knew that. She knew it wasn't a big deal necessarily, knew that the small piece of knowledge wasn't any real indication of anything. It didn't matter one way or the other if she owned one. Gabe probably assumed that she didn't have one because few New Yorkers did.

But for some reason, the seemingly insignificant detail served to draw attention to the fact that there was a part of Rachel's life—a glaringly large part—that Gabe knew nothing about. And no matter how the two of them proceeded from here, their relationship would always be founded on a lie. She hadn't been honest about where she worked or why she was in Philadelphia. The only thing she'd been truly candid about were her feelings for him. Though she worried that they wouldn't be, she hoped they would be enough.

"Can you take a look at this car I found if I walk around it with the phone?" Camille asked.

"Um . . . I guess I can try. Am I just saying if I like it or not? Because Rachel's here too, so you can get two opinions for the price of one."

"Oh. Hi, Rachel," Camille said with a wave when Gabe spun the phone toward her. "And no, to answer your question. I actually need you to look at the engine or whatever people look at to tell if cars are okay to buy."

"I thought you said the car was new?" Gabe asked.

"I said I was getting a new car. And it *is* new. To me. To someone else, it's a nine-year-old sedan they probably couldn't wait to get rid of. Come on, Gabriel. You think I could afford something brand-new?"

Gabe laughed. "Gotcha. Well, I'll try to see if anything looks weird, but I don't know if I'll be able to tell on a phone. Do you know how many miles it has on it?"

"Hang on," Camille said. Rachel heard her open the car door and then say, "A hundred and thirty-two thousand, six hundred and sixty-eight."

"Keep looking," Gabe told her. "That thing's gonna be joining Molly in the afterlife pretty soon."

"Really? How many miles should be on there?"

"I was hoping you'd tell me it had under a hundred thousand. Ten thousand a year is usually expected, so whoever owned that car first drove well over that."

"Oh, okay. Well, it smells like cat urine and patchouli in here anyway, so I'm not heartbroken about having to find something else."

Gabe made a disgusted face before asking her why she hadn't even looked inside yet.

"I looked in the windows to see the condition of the interior, but I didn't sit in it or drive it or anything. I knew I was gonna call you, so if you were gonna say it was a piece of shit—which you basically just did—I'd rather find out before I get too attached."

"Huh," Gabe said, looking impressed by Camille's explanation. "That's actually a pretty good idea. And I don't know that it's *definitely* a piece of shit, but it's got too many miles on it to risk it. In my opinion, at least. I bet you can find something better. Why don't you wait till tomorrow to look again, and I'll go with you, if you want?"

"Yeah, okay. That'd be awesome. You don't mind?"

"No. Not at all. I don't have a lot going on tomorrow, so I have time. I'd be happy to help."

The two said goodbye and Gabe told Camille he'd text her tomorrow morning and they'd figure out their plans.

"You don't mind if I go with Camille, do you?" Gabe asked Rachel after hanging up.

"No." Rachel was surprised he'd ask that. "Why would I mind?"

Gabe shrugged. "I know you aren't in the city much longer, so our time together is limited, that's all. But it shouldn't take all day or anything, so we could get together later, if you're free."

"Yeah, that's good," she said. "I have some work to get done anyway. You go help Camille, and you can text me when you get back. You said the other day Camille had a new girlfriend you hadn't met yet. Maybe we can call Jace and Aly and we can all hang out."

"Sounds like a plan," Gabe replied.

CHAPTER TWENTY-TWO

GABE

Sitting at his large desk with his head propped up by his hand cradling it at the temple, Gabe tried to finish up what seemed to be an endless pile of purchase orders and vendor bills. What he really needed was a secretary to help get him organized. It always felt like he was simply restacking things into different piles around his office. The clutter made his brain overwhelmed.

His phone buzzed, making his heart leap a little. What this shitty day needed was Rachel. Talking to her would definitely improve his mood.

But when he looked down at the screen, he saw a number he didn't recognize. He ignored it—and the disappointment— and refocused on his work. The phone stopped only to immediately start up again. And again after he ignored it for a second time. Somehow, the consistent buzz of his phone echoed louder in the quiet room than a ring would have. Gabe picked up the phone and looked at it for a second before giving into temptation and accepting the call. "Gabe Torres."

There was silence for a beat before a throat cleared. "Hi. Gabe. Uh, wow, sorry. I know I called you, but I guess I hadn't thought of what to actually say when you answered."

"Well, you can start by telling me who's calling," Gabe said.

"Oh, shit. Yeah, it's, uh, it's Cole Barnes."

Gabe leaned back in his chair and rubbed his forehead with his free hand. *Why the fuck did I answer the phone?* "What can I do for you, Cole?"

"I . . ." A large sigh whooshed out of the man. "I just wanted to apologize. Make amends for being such a dick."

Well, this wasn't what Gabe had expected. He hadn't heard from Cole in a couple months and had hoped the guy had disappeared off the face of the earth. But he sounded sincere, so while Gabe was skeptical, he figured there was no harm in hearing him out. "Okay," Gabe replied because he wasn't sure what else to say.

"Seriously, man, I was out of control. I don't even know why I was so fixated on getting back into the club. It was like once the thought popped into my brain, I started treating it like a crusade. Maybe I figured I could focus on that instead of what a disaster my life was becoming."

Gabe opened his mouth a couple of times but couldn't make a coherent thought form on his tongue. He finally forced out a, "You all good now?"

Cole sighed again. "I'm getting there. It's going to be hard to stay in recovery after all the years of partying I've done, but . . . I need to do it. I don't want my kids to remember me as some asshole who fucked up their lives. They deserve better. Better than me for sure, but I'm what they got stuck with, so I need to get my shit together." There was a hint of a joke in his tone when he said the last sentence, but there was also a sadness.

"It's cool, man. I hope it all works out for you. No hard feelings."

"Wow. Really? I thought for sure you'd wanna put my head through a wall after what I did."

Gabe laughed. "I was pretty annoyed. Threatening to go public about the club was pretty shitty, but at least you didn't go through with it."

The silence on the other end of the phone made Gabe increasingly anxious as it stretched on. "You didn't go through with it, right?"

"I was sure you would've heard by now. The guy at *All Access* seemed excited about it."

"*All Access*? As in *All Access Sports*? Are you fucking kidding me, you asshole!" Being sensitive and forgiving was forgotten as Gabe let his anger pour out. "What the fuck is your problem?"

"Oxys, cocaine, and whiskey. Among other things," Cole replied with the serene voice of someone who'd already confronted his demons and decided it was time to move on to the next phase of his life.

It pissed Gabe off. "That's great that you're so calm, dickhead. You may have sunk this whole place. Everything Mike worked for, everything he sacrificed—"

"You think you're telling me something I don't know? Something I haven't regretted since I went into treatment?" There was a hint of steel behind his voice that hadn't been there before. Seemed Cole still had some fire in him after all. "The only thing I can do is apologize. Whether you accept that or not is up to you."

Gabe groaned and pushed a hand through his short hair. "I have a contingency on my forgiveness," he finally said.

"What's that?"

"I can forgive you if you promise to never talk to me again. You are one pain in the ass I never want to feel again."

"Are there other pains in the ass you do want to feel?" Cole asked, humor lacing his voice.

"Fuck off, man," Gabe replied, though he knew his smile could be heard in his tone.

Cole laughed. "No problem. I can definitely fuck off. And for what it's worth, if they haven't sent that reporter woman to talk to you yet, they probably figured I was too unreliable a source to build a story on."

The back of Gabe's next prickled. It was a silly connection for his brain to make. There was no way it could be her, but he couldn't help asking about it anyway. "Do you know what the reporter's name was that they were supposed to send?"

"Eh, I'm not sure. She left me a voicemail once, but I deleted it. Began with an R, I think. Rebecca or... Renee? Fuck, I don't know."

Gabe's stomach dropped. "You don't happen to remember a last name, do you?"

"Nah, I'm not sure he ever even said. And if he did, there's no way I'd remember it. I could probably ask if—"

"No, no," Gabe interrupted. "It's cool. I'll just keep an eye out for a woman with a name beginning with R." The words felt sour on his tongue. There had to be a logical explanation for all this shit. But he couldn't think logically while he was still talking to Cole fucking Barnes. "Thanks for the apology, man. Best of luck."

"Thanks, Gabe. You too."

Gabe hung up quickly and dropped his phone onto his desk. He propped his elbows on it and let his head drop into his hands. This couldn't be happening. There was no way Rachel could be the reporter they sent to investigate the club. She'd never do that to him.

Would she?

Because the more Gabe thought about it, the more he convinced himself that he shouldn't be so sure. Rachel had shown up in Philly right around when the shit was Cole was going on. And she'd never actually told him who she was working for, had she? Or did she and he just didn't remember? Gabe racked his memory, trying to remember if she'd ever said, and concluded that she hadn't. And what did he really know about her? They hadn't spoken in ten years. She could be a serial killer for all he knew. Well, maybe a serial killer was a stretch, but he couldn't ignore the fact that she could be an accomplished liar who was getting off on messing with him. Just because he didn't *think* it was true didn't mean it wasn't.

It was all so fucked up. He snatched his phone up and went to her number. He found her name. There was nothing to do but ask her. She'd tell him the truth, right?

But if she'd been lying this entire time, she could easily lie to him now. And if she wasn't from *All Access,* she might never forgive him for thinking she'd do that to him. He thought about what to do for the rest of the afternoon, completely ignoring the work he promised to himself he'd get done.

Finally, a plan came to him. It was time to investigate the investigator.

CHAPTER TWENTY-THREE

RACHEL

Rachel had been stressing out over this damn story. The more she uncovered, the more people she talked to, the less she wanted to write it at all. There was no way around it. This story was going to destroy her relationship with Gabe. Her interview with Jamie Privy had solidified the fact that not only was there a club, but it was definitely located in Philadelphia. Then seeing Gabe with the cards . . . . It all led Rachel to a conclusion she didn't like one bit.

Rachel could refuse to write the story. She knew that was a completely plausible option that would get her out of the mess she found herself in. But she also knew that would be career suicide. Because for as nice of a guy Rick was, he demanded professionalism. Not to mention the fact that he had his own bosses to answer to. If she didn't come through after all the resources they'd spent keeping her in Philly, she'd be out on her ass with a trail of bad references chasing after her. And she'd spent most of her career chasing this story. It would've basically reduced the last ten years to nothing.

She *hated* to think that she was choosing her job over Gabe. It made her sick to know that, by writing this story, that's the decision she was making. But the relationship with Gabe was new. There were no guarantees there. He could decide tomorrow that he was over her and move on. While part of her understood how unlikely that was because the same part of her *knew* Gabe—knew what kind of man he was and how he felt about her—another part screamed at her to get the job done and accomplish a goal that had been ten years in the making. It had taken years of slogging through copy and writing fluff pieces that ended up on the cutting-room floor. Dozens of bullshit assignments and failed leads had led her to this story: the one that could make her entire career.

Not writing this story would feel like a slap in the face to everything she'd fought through and for. It would be like reaching a finish line and then turning around and running back the way she'd come. It would be a failure, and there'd be no one to blame for it but herself.

Rachel didn't know how to choose between the two most important things in her life. So she decided to go with what seemed to be less of a gamble and hoped that when the bottom fell out of this thing with Gabe, that he'd one day be able to forgive her. Though she knew that was probably a long shot.

She also knew that she needed to tell him. There was no way she could let him find out when the story hit the paper. He was at least owed that much. Today. She'd tell him today. Before she had time to chicken out.

Rachel grabbed her phone off the coffee table to call Gabe, but it dinged in her hand before she could pull up his number. Coincidentally, it was a text from Gabe.

Hey, you around? I thought you might
want to come over, and I'll order us a late
lunch/early dinner.

A sinking feeling in the pit of her stomach made her nauseous. For the first time since she could remember, she didn't want to see Gabe, even though she knew she had to. She'd just walk in there and tell him—like ripping off a Band-Aid. Then he'd kick her out, and she'd be depressed for a while. Maybe years, but it wouldn't be anything she didn't deserve.

> *Sure, I can be there in a half hour.*
> *Does that work?*

Perfect

She threw the phone on the couch and practiced some deep breathing exercises. She could do this. *Would* do this. She grabbed her stuff and went downstairs to hail a cab. Traffic was picking up in the city, but she still managed to get there a few minutes early. By the time she made it to Gabe's door, he was standing at it waiting for her.

"Hey," he said with a soft smile that was a little dimmer than the one he usually shone on her. He opened the door wider so she could walk in and then closed it behind him. "I'm sorry to do this, but Jace just called and asked if I could help him at the hospital. Aly has a new patient that's evidently a baseball fan." He maintained his smile but seemed to be avoiding her eyes, though it was probably because he felt bad canceling.

"I know you wanted to come to my volunteer outings, but I don't think this is a good time for that," he explained, which made Rachel feel like a jerk that Gabe would think she'd want to gawk at him while he helped a sick child.

"I totally understand," she replied.

"It'll take me no more than two hours," he continued. "I thought that, since you came all the way over here, you'd maybe wanna hang out and wait for me? Then I can take you out for dinner to make it up to you." Gabe said the words in such a soft way, it made her heart flutter. The fact that he wanted her to wait for him was endearing.

"Sure. I'm free for the rest of the day, so I can definitely hang out."

He shoved his hands in his pockets and smiled at her again. "Great." He picked up his key ring and looked down at it. "I called for a car, so I don't need my keys." He held them out to her. "Why don't you hang on to them in case you decide you want to step out for a bit? That way you can lock up and get back in."

She gingerly took the keys from him. Warning bells sounded in her mind as the journalist in her knew what this could mean. He was leaving his keys with her. She'd have access to whatever these keys opened. And maybe he had another set of keys for the club, but there was still a *chance*. "Okay," she said. "Thanks."

He nodded. "No problem. See you in a couple of hours." Then he opened the door and was gone, leaving her alone in his apartment with his keys.

She looked around as she let her fingers rub over the metal. The main issue was—aside from the fact that she was a horrible person for even considering this—she didn't know exactly where the club was.

Or did she?

She pulled her phone from her pocket and went into her email to find the one Jared had sent. The one she'd never opened because she was a good person who didn't want to pry into the personal business of her boyfriend. The truth was, she was way beyond that now, probably had been from the beginning. She'd been lying to him from the start. She was the villain in this story. She might as well go all the way.

She skimmed the information that included a credit history and his social security number, until she came to properties he owned. And there's where she found an address for a property in Philly that wasn't the one she was currently standing in. She grabbed her purse and Gabe's keys and ran out the door to put the final pieces of the puzzle into place.

She tracked down a cab and gave the driver the address. As he drove her away from Gabe's part of the city and into a decidedly more run-down section, she looked down at the email and then out the window, her brows furrowing in confusion. *This can't be right.* "Are you sure this is the way to 578 Espiar Street?"

"Yes, ma'am," he replied.

About ten minutes later, and in an even more decrepit part of the city, the cab pulled over to the curb. "Here we are," the driver said.

Rachel looked around. They were in front of a building that had an alley leading down the right side. The windows were boarded up, and it looked like it hadn't been occupied in years. "Can you wait?" she asked.

"Absolutely."

Taking a deep breath, Rachel pushed open the car door and walked up to the building. There was a door, but it was blocked by wood that had been nailed over it. Pursing her lips, she wondered what the hell this place was. She walked to the corner of the building and looked down the alley. With one last look at the cab, she started making her way down the narrow, concrete space. Even though the sun was still high in the sky, the towering building on either side of her plunged the alley into shadow. It was creepy and scary, and she wanted to be out of there yesterday. But still she walked until she arrived at a large fire door. "Here goes nothing," she whispered to herself.

She held the keys up to the door and began trying them in the lock. Finally, she got to one that pushed in easily, but she stopped herself before turning it. Tears sprang to her eyes, and as she tried to blink them back, they began to fall down her cheeks. What the hell was wrong with her? She was here. She'd already committed the ultimate betrayal. What difference did it make if she went inside? The damage was done.

A shudder worked through her as she stood there, holding the key in the lock with a trembling hand. "Fuck," she whispered.

Rachel wasn't sure why *this* was the thing that felt too far, but it was. This was the hurdle she couldn't—wouldn't—jump. She hadn't known it until right this second, but she could *not* do this to Gabe. Because everything she knew now was still hypothetical. Without *seeing* a club, there could always be plausible deniability that there was one. But if she went inside...

Granted, she could always deny she'd gone in. She could go take a look around, find out the truth for herself to satisfy her curiosity. She'd always *know* she could've written the story, but that she'd *chosen* not to.

For Gabe.

But she owed him so much more than that. She owed him not to completely obliterate his life.

Letting out a deep breath she hadn't even been aware she'd been holding, she made her decision. She went to slide the key out of the lock when a voice spoke behind her.

"Congratulations. I guess you've finally found what you were looking for."

CHAPTER TWENTY-FOUR

GABE

"Gabe, I—"

Gabe interrupted whatever she was about to say by grabbing the key from her and opening the door himself. He'd hoped this wouldn't be how it all played out. He hoped that she'd just hang out in his apartment and wait for him and it wouldn't be true that she was investigating him and the club.

He'd worried that even if she was the one investigating the club that she wouldn't know where it was and he'd still have doubts about who she was. But as he'd followed her here in his car—using his spare key—it had quickly become clear that he didn't have to worry about that. It also became impossible to deny that everything he thought he knew about Rachel was about to collapse around him. "Go ahead," he said as he gestured her through the doorway.

She didn't move, tears streaming down her face as she looked at him, the dark hall, then back at him. "Please, let me explain."

"What's there to explain? You came here for a story. It's in there," he told her as he pointed inside.

She stared at him for a second before she walked into the

hallway that led to the club. It was lined with boxes and skids, intentionally left to look like an abandoned building so that even if someone got this far, they likely wouldn't see a point in going farther.

Gabe flicked on the light. "It's at the end of the hall through another set of fire doors." He was working hard to keep his voice even, controlled. Letting her know how angry he was, how hurt, wasn't something he was willing to do. He'd shown her enough of himself already, and gotten nothing but lies in return.

"You don't have to do this," she said, her voice almost a whisper. "You don't have to show me anything."

"Don't act like you gave me a choice. *You* brought us here, to this. There's only going forward from here."

She swiped at her cheeks with her hand before making her way down the hall. When they arrived at the other set of heavy fire doors, Gabe unlocked them and pushed them open. He paused, steeling himself for what would come next. The reality setting in of what he'd cost everyone associated with the Players' Club, simply because he'd fallen in love with a girl who'd only pretended to love him back. He heaved the doors open and held them so she could walk through.

Her head swiveled around the space, taking everything in. Gabe joined her, reminding himself how great he'd thought this place was when he first saw it. How great it *still* was, even though he'd ruined it.

After a few minutes, she turned back to him. "It's beautiful."

He felt an eyebrow quirk at that. As if her compliments about the place she was going to destroy with a few taps to a keyboard meant shit now.

She looked abashed, and her eyes darted away from his as she turned her back to him. "I'm sorry," she croaked.

He pondered that for a moment. "For which part?"

Turning back to him, her eyes found his. "All of it."

He leaned back against the bar and folded his arms across his chest. "So, now you've seen it. Want to interview me about it? Maybe have me give you a list of members so I can completely destroy every shred of credibility I have?"

"I wasn't going to come in, Gabe. I swear."

Gabe couldn't help the harsh laugh that left his throat. "You swear? Are you for real right now? You think you 'swearing' means anything to me? You've done nothing but lie since the Super Bowl."

"That isn't true. It wasn't *all* a lie."

"Do you hear yourself? It wasn't *all* a lie? None of it should've been a lie." He straightened, and his voice was getting louder with every sentence he spoke despite his trying his best to keep his cool.

"I know. You're right. You're so right. But I need you to understand that the story was completely separate from everything else. From how I felt—"

"Goddamn it, *I* was the story," he yelled as he slammed his hand down on the bar top. She jumped slightly, and he felt a twinge of remorse for startling her until he remembered that he was the one who'd been betrayed. "The two were never separate. How could they be?"

"Because I didn't know. I didn't know you owned the club."

Gabe scoffed.

"It's true," Rachel argued. "Running into you when I got here was a total coincidence. I had no idea you were involved until I saw the bank statement at your house."

Gabe looked down at the floor and shook his head. This was the type of conversation that could go around in circles for hours. And while Gabe had once thought he'd want to do nothing more than spend hours talking with Rachel, now he was just tired. Tired of arguing, tired of trying to figure out what the truth was, tired of hurting. It was all too much. "I can't do this."

Rachel's eyes found his, and their red rims showed how sorry she was. Or did they? Maybe it was time Gabe realized that he didn't know her at all. This woman in front of him was a stranger—a stranger he needed to be done with.

"I'm so sorry, Gabe."

"I can believe that," he said on a sigh. "But it doesn't change anything." Gesturing toward the exit, Gabe told her, "I think it's time you left."

Rachel opened her mouth to reply and then seemed to think better of it. She nodded once and walked to the doors. Still facing them, she said, "For what it's worth, knowing you has been the best thing that's happened to me in a long time. Goodbye, Gabe." She pushed the doors open and was gone before he could reply. Not that he would've.

But now, alone in his club with no one to hear but the immortalizations of former players on the walls, he said the last words he'd ever say to her. "Bye, Rachel."

CHAPTER TWENTY-FIVE

GABE

"This is the saddest sight I've ever seen."

Gabe lifted his head to see who had spoken, even though he already knew the voice. "Hey," he said to Jace. Gabe went back to polishing the bar top. "To what do I owe the pleasure?"

Jace pulled out a bar stool and sat down. "What? I can't just stop by and see my best friend?"

Gabe looked up long enough to shoot him a skeptical look.

"Okay, fine," Jace said. "I talked to Ben," he added softly. "Why didn't you tell me about Rachel?"

Gabe cleared his throat. "I only felt like telling the story once." And wasn't that the damn truth. Gabe had needed to vent to someone—expel the whole story as if it were poison in his body. But once it was out there, all he'd felt was empty. He hadn't wanted to speak of it since.

"I'm not trying to get all emo teenager on you, but why'd you tell Ben and not me? He's not even here to help you out."

Gabe inhaled deeply and set his rag down before dropping his forearms onto the bar. "I think that's why I chose him. I wanted to tell someone, but I didn't want to have to look that person in the face afterward."

Gabe dipped his head, but Jace lowered his own to catch Gabe's eyes. "Why?"

Gabe scoffed. "What the fuck do you mean 'why'? Why would I? I got played by a reporter. That shit is embarrassing."

"I'm your boy. You should never be embarrassed to tell me anything."

"Don't give me that Dr. Phil bullshit. If I'm embarrassed, I'm embarrassed. There's no changing how I feel."

"Come on. You've seen both me and Ben fuck up relationships. This is no different."

"It's completely different," Gabe yelled.

"How?"

"Because *you* fucked those up. You and Ben brought all that shit on yourselves. All I did was love some girl who couldn't give a fuck less about me. There's no mistake for me to fix. No apologies to give. I can't make this right because I didn't screw it up in the first place."

Jace sat back, watching Gabe. Whether it was because he didn't know what to say or figured Gabe had more words in him, Gabe wasn't sure.

Looking around, Gabe gave a humorless laugh. "You know I thought this place was going to make everything better. I was losing baseball whether I wanted to or not. My body just couldn't hack it anymore. And I kept wondering what I was going to do with myself afterward. I convinced myself that I was ready to leave the game. That it was my choice to be done. But it wasn't. My body decided it for me."

Jace sighed. "Why didn't you tell us?"

"Tell you what? That I was scared to death?" Gabe shook his head. "You know that's not me, Jace. I'm the life of the party, not the wimp who's afraid of life after baseball because he never *envisioned* a life after baseball."

"There's no role you have to fill here. We're not your fans. You don't need to portray a character for us. We're your best friends."

Gabe knew that. He did. But it didn't change anything for him. He'd spent most of his life putting on a face to hide his true feelings. While Ben and Jace knew him better than anyone else, there was always something that stopped Gabe from going all in. From opening all the way up so they could see the deepest parts of him. The only person he'd ever been that honest with was Rachel, and look where that had gotten him. But as he looked at Jace, he knew he could tell the man anything. Jace would never think less of him. It was time Gabe trusted him. "I'm fucking lonely, man. I thought this place would fill in the empty cracks, but it didn't. It only made them worse. And while a part of me loves this place, part of me hates it now too."

"What do you hate most about it?" Jace asked.

Gabe took his time replying, wanting to give the most honest answer he could. "The drama. It's like nightmare on top of nightmare sometimes. It's not even the time I have to dedicate to it, because that kind of ebbs and flows. But, Christ, it's been one headache after another ever since I took over."

"What do you love most about it?" Jace asked next as he leaned forward in his seat.

Taking a deep breath, Gabe said, "It gives me roots. My mom sent me from Puerto Rico so I could have a future, and professional baseball traded me all over the league. But this place is my responsibility. It makes me feel tied to a place for the first time in a long time."

"You wanna know what I think?"

"Not really," Gabe replied, which set them both off laughing. Which was a relief. Gabe desperately needed to feel a little more like himself.

"I think the drama will fade. It's growing pains. You'll get used to operating this place, and it'll all become second nature to you. The roots, they're forever. They're worth hanging in there for." Jace let his eyes roam around the club for a minute before continuing. "There's a lot of life in this place, a lot of good times. But there are a lot of secrets too. You'll need to be prepared for how hard it'll be to have a personal life and still run this place."

Gabe smiled, but it was sad. "Guess I don't have to worry about that now, do I?"

Jace looked at him sympathetically as he rubbed a hand over his head. "What do you think she'll do?"

"I think she'll write her story. It's what she came here to do, and there's nothing stopping her from it."

Jace looked doubtful at Gabe's words.

"What?" Gabe asked.

"I just... I don't know. I guess I think there's more stopping her than you think."

"Is this where we hold hands and you promise me her love was real?"

"Well, I mean, I'd rather not hold your hand," Jace joked.

Gabe laughed but sobered quickly. "There's not a whole lot I can do about it either way. Either she writes it and destroys the club, or she doesn't. But I have to worry that she will for the rest of my life. There's not exactly a winning situation here."

"And you and her are...?"

"Done. There's no way someone who could manipulate me like that has any genuine feelings for me. At least none that

I'd ever be able to trust."

Jace nodded. "I get that." He was silent a moment longer before he rubbed his hand over the half-polished bar top. "You want help with this bar? At the rate you're going, it'll never get cleaned."

Gabe threw a rag at him. "It would've if some asshole hadn't come to distract me."

And the two spent the rest of the afternoon cleaning up the mess that was Gabe's bar and his life.

CHAPTER TWENTY-SIX

RACHEL

Rachel stared out the window at the bustling city below. She couldn't even have told anyone what she was thinking about. She was simply letting the city—and all that had happened there—wash through her. It was a polarizing experience, with such incredible highs and drastic lows. But she knew that anytime she came back to Philadelphia, the predominant feelings would be overwhelming regret and unutterable sadness.

"How is it possible that you have even more shit now than when you left New York?" Kellan asked as he walked back into her apartment after taking some boxes down to the small moving van she'd rented.

She shrugged, not able to put into words how she actually felt like she was leaving Philly with nothing. Yes, she had the story she went there for, but the sacrifice outweighed its value.

Kellan walked over and grabbed her shoulders so he could turn her to face him. "I need you to stop acting like a pod person. It's freaking me the hell out, and I'm not interested in sharing my apartment with an alien."

"It's my apartment."

"There she is," he replied with a smile, though he quickly let it drop. "It'll be okay. You'll see. Once we get you home, and you get back into your routine, you'll forget all about what's-his-name."

"Gabe," she answered.

Kellan rolled his eyes. "I knew his name. I was trying to make a joke."

She stared back at him blankly, letting him know the joke had missed its mark. "I hurt him. Really badly," she said.

"I know."

"And I can't fix it. Because even if I don't write the story, he'll never forgive me anyway. So not writing it will be a waste of everything I sacrificed."

"You trying to convince me or yourself?" he asked.

She shrugged him off. "What am I supposed to do? Seriously, I need you to tell me what to do."

He leaned his hip against the wall. "You know what to do."

"Stop being all Yoda-esque. I need advice. I don't know what to do." Her voice cracked at the end of her sentence, and tears began to fall.

Wrapping his arms around her, Kellan pulled her close. "You do know what to do. You've probably known for weeks. You just haven't wanted to do it."

She burrowed her head into his chest before the need to breathe forced her to turn her head. "I don't want to ruin my career. I worked so hard for it."

"Just like Gabe worked hard for his?"

Rachel pulled back quickly. "What do you mean?"

"Come on, Rach. You're a smart girl. This was always going to destroy someone. Yeah, it's really bad fucking karma that it happened to be the guy you liked, but you were always going to hurt somebody. You were always going to end someone's livelihood. The only one you've tried to protect all this time was yourself."

"That's not true," she protested.

"Of course it is. And I'm not judging you for it. I'm one of the most selfish people on the planet, so if that's the road you want to walk down, I'll hop in and we can carpool down that bitch. But don't pretend like you never had a choice. You've been the only one with choices this entire time."

"But this story—"

"Stop with the story, Rachel. This isn't about a story. It's about your life, and what you can live with and what you can't."

She looked back out the window and let Kellan's words sink in. This *was* about her life. What she'd dedicated herself to. The goals she'd set. The priorities she held.

Looking back at Kellan, she whispered, "I've got to write the story."

"Then let's get you home so you can get started."

★ ★ ★

A week later, Rachel stood in Rick's office as he read over the piece she'd written. When he finished, he set his glasses down, interlaced his fingers as he rested them on his belly, and looked up at her. "You're sure you want to go ahead with this?"

Rachel had needed to give him at least a vague rundown about what had led her to this story. If there was any backlash about any unethical behavior on her part, she wanted the magazine to be prepared to handle it. Not that she thought Gabe would make a complaint against her. Maybe it was more that it felt like a confession. No absolution could be granted, but there was still peace in the telling. "Yeah. I'm sure."

"Okay. You got it in just in time for it to go in the June publication."

Rachel nodded.

Rick shuffled some things around on his desk. "Your request for leave was granted. Any idea when you'll be ready to come back?"

"I figured I'd see how the story was received and evaluate my options then."

Rick took a deep breath. "Well, we'll miss you around here."

Rachel laughed. "I haven't stepped foot in this office in months. It'll be business as usual for you guys."

Rick returned her smile. "I guess that's true. In that case, get the hell out of here. The rest of us have work to do."

Rolling her eyes with a chuckle, Rachel extended her hand. "Thank you, Rick. For everything."

Rick stood and grasped her hand. "My pleasure. I hope the next couple of months lead you to wherever you need to be."

"Me too." She gave his hand one final shake before leaving his office. She looked around at all the chaos in the room: the bustling of reporters, the ringing of phones, the streaming of press conferences. She knew she'd miss it over the following months, but she also knew this time was important to her for a number of reasons.

The story about Gabe's club had taken a lot out of her, both in the investigating and in the actual writing. And what she'd put together could cause a fair bit of backlash. It was best that she give herself time to mentally and emotionally recover before she found herself thrust into whatever maelstrom this story might create.

Rachel left the building, putting on her sunglasses as she stepped out into the bright May afternoon. The sunshine felt good as it warmed her face. She let herself bask in it for a moment before she got caught up in the throng of New Yorkers rushing from place to place.

She found solace in the fact that she wouldn't have to rush anything for a little while. For once, she'd stop being on the chase and let come what may.

CHAPTER TWENTY-SEVEN

GABE

Gabe popped behind the bar to check on the bartenders and see if they needed anything restocked. They said they were in good shape so Gabe turned to mingle, but before he got far, he heard a voice call out to him. He turned to see Manny walking toward him. The serious expression on his face caused Gabe to tense up. Manny tossed a magazine on top of the bar and leaned over it.

"Gabe, you seen this yet?"

Gabe took a couple steps so that he was directly across the bar from Manny. "Seen what?"

Flipping through the magazine, Manny said, "That girl you were talking to. Rachel? She wrote something I thought you might want to see."

Gabe's entire body seized as panic filled him. *She wrote it.* It had been two months since he'd confronted Rachel at the club. Two months of replaying their time together, of analyzing every word and action, of driving himself insane because no matter how many times he tried to convince himself their relationship had all been a ruse, it sure as hell *felt* real.

It had also been enough time that he'd begun to believe

that she wouldn't publish the story. That she wouldn't completely betray him. But he should've known better than to let himself hope for anything where she was concerned.

Manny turned the magazine around so Gabe could read it. He had to will himself to look down at the glossy pages. When he did, his eyes narrowed as soon as they rested on the title. Pulling the magazine closer to him, Gabe said, "Rachel wrote this?"

Manny flashed a small smile. "That's her name and picture under the headline, isn't it?"

When he let his eyes drift below the title, he saw that it was. A small, unwanted thrill shot through him at seeing her picture. "Can I borrow this?"

Manny nodded, his smile growing. "Sure thing. I don't need it back."

As he walked, Gabe looked at the front cover to see the words *All Access Sports* written on the cover with "June Edition" in smaller letters underneath. The magazine had clearly just come out. Gabe hurried to his office and locked the door behind him. He dropped into his chair and hunched forward over his desk as he opened back to the page his index finger had been holding, and began to read.

THE RIGHT TO BE

BY RACHEL ADLER

I've spent ten years investigating the harsh reality that is the modern sports world. Ten years of interviewing athletes who've endured countless injuries, been exposed to devastating criticism, and been lambasted for not living up to expectations— both personally and professionally.

I have given the public what I felt they were owed: an inside look into every facet of the men and women who have risen to near superhero status. There was never a story that was too inappropriate, too sensational, too private. It was never a matter of hovering as close to some mythical ethical line I was forbidden, as a journalist, to cross because there is no line. In the collective mind of society, athletes are public figures and therefore forced into a limelight that never dims.

But is this right? Is it fair?

Does it matter?

To players like Gabriel Torres, it does. Torres, a former shortstop for the Philadelphia Premiers, retired last fall after the demands of the game became too much for his body to endure. He was a fan favorite, someone who was often called upon to do special meet and greets with fans after games and to attend special events being held in the community.

But when he retired, he expected to get his life back. And not from whom you may think.

"To be honest, the fans don't recognize me much," Torres said. "I don't think they expect to see a former professional athlete out and about. The real concern is the media. They're everywhere, always looking for their next big story."

And often, that big story comes at the cost of the players' well-being.

Cole Barnes, a former NFL left tackle whose struggles with addiction have been well-documented since his retirement in 2014, also feels that he's thrust into the spotlight unjustly. "Don't get me wrong, I'm responsible for my own choices. But seeing every mistake I made splashed across the front page didn't help matters. I wasn't even playing anymore. I didn't get why it was even relevant to anyone."

Barnes brings up a valid point. Are the lives of former athletes relevant? Does signing a professional contract automatically grant the media access to every aspect of their lives forever?

Up until a few months ago, I thought it did. Many of us in the media are of the mind-set that the public has a right to know everything. So we put it all out there for them to decide what they want to read and what they don't. After all, these athletes signed up for this. Everyone knows that being a professional athlete entails having your life splayed across every news outlet whenever you get a speeding ticket or are associated with a disturbance that may or may not actually involve you.

Don't they?

"I signed my contract when I was twenty-two years old. I barely even read it," Torres said of his first contract with the Minneapolis Ravens. "All I knew was that it would get me in the Majors. I didn't care about anything else."

So many of these players are so overcome with emotion of being selected as one of the elite few chosen to enter the world of professional sports, they jump at the chance without thinking about all they will have to sacrifice.

Barnes told us, "My ex-wife told me not to come to my daughter's birthday party because all I ever did was bring a media circus with me wherever I went. Imagine that. Not being able to go to your kid's birthday because the paparazzi treats you like a sideshow act."

And I can actually imagine it, because I was—am—one of those reporters. Someone who would readily fight for my own right to privacy, but was quick to trample others when doing so would get me the scoop.

For ten years, I have been part of the problem. Most of us have been, not only members of the media, but of the public as well. The question is, how do we fix it?

Unfortunately, I don't have an answer for that. I'm hoping that bringing awareness to the issue will at least be a start, but I know better than to think it has absolved me of any of my previous misdeeds.

There are certain things that do not deserve to be forgiven. But that doesn't mean that we shouldn't repent.

Gabe finished reading and sank back into his chair. It definitely wasn't the article he'd been expecting, and he felt a wave of relief for it. She had enough information on him to bury the entire place. The fact that she hadn't done that made him feel like maybe not *everything* she'd said had been a lie. And damn, was that possibility appealing. It made him feel lighter in some way.

He pulled his phone out and looked at his text messages. Scrolling down, he eventually came to Rachel's name. He typed out *Thank you* and slid his thumb over to send it, but he hesitated.

This would be opening a door, a line of communication that Gabe wasn't sure he wanted open. Because sure, this article was great. It demonstrated her taking accountability for her actions and apologizing for them.

But it didn't change anything.

What they'd had—or what he thought they had—was gone. Or probably more precisely, it had never existed in the first place. It was best to let the past remain there.

Gabe clicked out of his text messages and stood up, sliding his phone in his pocket. He had a job to do, a future to work toward. And it was outside of his office door—not on the other end of a phone.

CHAPTER TWENTY-EIGHT

RACHEL

Rachel stepped out into the oppressive heat of a city she didn't think she'd ever find herself in again. At least not this soon. But duty called, so here she was.

The month since her article had come out had been... interesting. Initially, the higher-ups at *All Access Sports* hadn't been too happy with her—and they'd been even less happy with Rick for allowing the article to go to print. But as Rick and Rachel's bosses were debating whether to fire them or put them in the fact-checking department to toil away for the rest of their lives, something Rachel never foresaw happened.

Athletes from all over the country began calling. They had stories to tell and trusted that *All Access* would give them that opportunity without putting the media's spin on them. Some people even specifically requested Rachel. The magazine went from being on the brink of firing her to flying her all over the country to speak to athletes in a variety of sports and stages in their careers.

So here she was, back in Philadelphia, walking out of a small office building where she'd met with a local basketball player and his agent. His story, an airing out of the rumors surrounding his being paid by boosters in college, was an intriguing one, and she was excited to begin writing it. She looked around the neighborhood and realized she was actually quite close to Gabe's condo. It would be a long walk, but it could be walked.

Not that she was thinking of walking there. What purpose would that serve? She hadn't heard from him since their fight three months ago. Rachel wasn't even sure if he'd seen her article. The thought had crossed her mind to call and ask him, but she'd never gotten up the courage to dial his number.

But that didn't mean that she'd given up her feelings for him. She missed him every day. Memories of their time together would pop up randomly throughout the day, and she wished that those memories weren't tinged with the overwhelming guilt that always accompanied thoughts of Gabe. The idea that she'd always feel that way—that she'd never be able to fully appreciate what they'd shared because regret would always color their relationship—made a pit grow in her stomach.

Maybe that's what made her begin to walk in the direction of his place. She had no intention of going in or calling him, but she needed to be in his vicinity. Perhaps it would give her some clarity. Perhaps it would make her feel even worse. It was a toss-up. Whatever the reason she was turning into a stalker, she knew there was no stopping it. Once the seed had been planted, she couldn't resist.

She'd shored up her nerve as she walked, but it began to slip when she reached his block. She lowered her head and pulled her bag up higher on her shoulder as if she ridiculously thought she could disappear behind the strap. It was dusk, the sun descending behind the tall buildings that made up the city's skyline. Hopefully he wouldn't be able to tell it was her if he happened to catch a glimpse of her out one of his windows.

Part of her wanted to turn around, but she forced herself onward. This felt like something she needed to do, no matter how silly it might be. She expected to dart past his building, maybe take a glance at a place she'd never get to be again, murmur some form of a goodbye, and drift back into the throng of the city feeling like she could move past all of this.

But this was Rachel's life, so she probably shouldn't have had any such expectations.

She ducked her head as she approached the building, causing her to not see the solid chest of a man she smacked into as she all but sprinted past. Hands gripped her biceps, keeping her from bouncing off the guy like a rubber ball. She opened her mouth to mutter a quick, "Sorry," when the owner of the chest spoke.

"Rachel?"

Her head flew up as her eyes grew comically wide. "Oh shit," she blurted out before she could filter her words.

That earned her a smirk. "It's Jace, actually." But the smile quickly disappeared. "What are you doing here?" he asked, his tone serious, though not unkind.

Rachel stammered for a second before saying, "I honestly don't know."

Jace seemed to mull something over for a bit before he spoke again. "You gonna talk to him?"

Sighing, Rachel willed her body to relax. "I hadn't planned on it."

"Really? I figured you would have some things to say."

"Yeah, but I'm not sure he wants to hear them."

Pulling his phone out of his pocket, Jace held it up. "There's only one way to find out."

She knew he'd tell Gabe she'd been there, but he was giving her the choice to stick around for that call or to hightail it out of there. But maybe running into Jace was some kind of warped kismet. Maybe she owed Gabe—and herself—a conversation. Whether either of them wanted to have it or not. After thinking it over, she nodded, and Jace scrolled through his phone and made the call.

"Hey... Yeah, I know I just left... No, I didn't forget anything... No, I don't miss you already... Yes... Jesus Christ, will you shut up for a second!" Jace looked exasperated, but there was a fondness that was clear on his face. "I have someone down here who wants to talk to you... No, it's not a fan... Look, just come down, okay? I'm taking off."

Rachel shifted nervously. She wasn't prepared for this, but it appeared to be happening regardless.

Jace hung up the phone and looked at her. "Just do right by him, okay? He didn't deserve any of that shit."

Rachel nodded. "I know. I'll do my best."

He stared at her for a moment longer before nodding. "Take care, Rachel."

"You too."

He was already across the street climbing into his truck by the time Gabe came bounding out of his building. When his eyes rested on her, he stopped dead in his tracks before seeming to shore himself and approach her. Once he was in front of her, he shoved his hands in his pockets and rocked slowly on his heels. "Hey," he said. "Wasn't expecting to see you down here."

She smiled timidly. "I wasn't really expecting to be seen. But I'm glad I was. There are some things you deserve to hear." Despite believing what she said, Rachel had no idea where to begin. She hesitated, and silence stretched between them.

"I read your article," he said.

"Yeah? Good. I was hoping you had. Not that I wrote it just so you would… I mean, it wasn't just because… I needed…" She took a deep breath. "I wanted you to know where my head was at. What I learned. And I also didn't want you to be constantly worrying about an article about the club coming out."

"I appreciate that."

Tears burned her eyes. "I know I've already said this, but I'm so sorry, Gabe. I know it doesn't mean much to you now, but it's the only thing I have to offer."

"I accept your apology."

"Really?" He'd said it so easily, like his forgiving her was a foregone conclusion. It gave her a spark of hope she had no right to feel.

"I don't like holding on to hard feelings. It makes it impossible to move on, ya know?"

His words made her hope ignite like a moth in a flame, but she tried to hide it. "Thank you."

"Okay, well, I have some stuff to take care of. It was good seeing you, Rach. Take care of yourself." He turned to go back into his building, but she knew she couldn't let it happen. This would be her last chance to talk to him. She couldn't squander it.

"I don't regret it."

Gabe stopped short and slowly turned around. "What does that mean?" he said with an edge to his voice.

"I'm glad I came here to write the article. I wish I could change some of the circumstances, to have opened my eyes sooner to what I was losing by continuing, but I'll never be sorry my editor sent me here. Because, unknowingly, he was sending me to you."

Gabe sighed and opened his mouth to most likely dismiss her, so she plowed forward. "You were nowhere on my radar at first. The thought crossed my mind that you maybe knew about the club, but my getting close to you had nothing to do with that. Even when I saw the bank statement, I tried to look for other avenues to prove the club existed so the lines between us wouldn't blur. I hoped finding out you were somehow involved with the club would just be a stepping stone toward finding a bigger fish."

He scoffed. "I can't tell you how great it feels to have you call me a stepping stone."

"I'd rather be honest and have you hate me than lie to you anymore."

He didn't respond to that other than to cross his arms over his chest, which she took as an indication to continue. "When it started to become clear that you were the bigger fish, I told myself that my objective had changed. Now, my goal was to prove that you weren't involved. I pretended like my cause was noble, that I was trying to clear you of some huge scandal. See, you weren't the only one I was lying to. I did a number on myself too."

"Is that supposed to make me feel better?" he asked.

"I'm not trying to make you feel anything. I never was. I wasn't trying to trick you into caring about me." Rachel wasn't sure how to explain what was in her heart. How did one put words to something so visceral? "If I could take anything back, it would be you falling for me. Because I know you loved me. It was in every look you gave me and every moment we spent together. But I don't deserve it. Don't deserve *you*. And those aren't just words. It's something I know. I know it, and I wish it weren't true because I don't think I'll ever love somebody like I love you. And I lost it because I wasn't worthy of it. I'm still not. But that's my burden to carry. I'm sorry that I also made it yours."

Gabe stood there for what felt like a long time before he spoke. "I don't know what to say."

"You don't need to say anything. You don't owe me any words. I'm the one with the debt to pay."

Pushing a hand through his hair, Gabe looked lost. She'd wanted to make things better for him, but it seemed like she'd only made it worse. He dropped his hand to his side. "I wasn't always honest with you either. Some of the volunteer stuff I said I was doing, I made a lot of that shit up. I mean, I *have* gone to the hospital with Jace to visit kids, but that's not a regular thing for me. And I don't even like dogs, let alone invite them into my house. And now I live with two fucking cats that terrorize me."

A chuckle escaped Rachel. "I'm pretty sure on the scale of mistruths, you rank pretty low."

Gabe returned her laugh, but sobered quickly. "I don't really though, do I? Because while your lie totally sucked my heart right out of me, the fact is, if we'd stayed together, I'd have lied to you for the rest of our lives. I don't think I would've ever told you about the club, and maybe… Hell, I don't know." Gabe pushed a hand through his hair. "Maybe we were always going to break up, ya know? Either because of your lie or mine. There's no way to build a strong foundation when you aren't being honest with the other person."

His words weren't a revelation to her. She'd thought the same thing on a few occasions. She was definitely the more duplicitous, but neither of them had been in a position to give their relationship staying power. "Yeah. You're probably right." She looked down at the sidewalk before continuing. "Thanks for hearing me out."

Gabe nodded. "I think we both needed it." They looked at one another for a second before Gabe spoke. "You need me to call you a cab or anything?" he offered because he was Gabe and sweet all the way through.

"No, that's okay. I'm actually staying at the Hyatt not far from here."

"Oh, good. Yeah, that's only like three blocks that way," he said as he pointed down the street.

They stood there silently until Gabe stepped forward awkwardly and wrapped an arm around her shoulder. She let herself sink into the embrace a little. The moment felt final, and she wanted to enjoy it. "I wish you all the best," he said into her ear. "I really mean that."

He pulled back, and she wrapped her arms around her stomach. It was a poor replacement for Gabe's comforting embrace. "Thank you. You too."

He offered her one more smile before walking back to his building and disappearing inside.

Rachel stood on the sidewalk and tried not to drop to the ground at the sight of Gabe walking away from her so easily. Instead, she focused on putting one foot in front of the other, and hoping that, with time, she'd be able to move on too.

CHAPTER TWENTY-NINE

GABE

Gabe walked back to his condo, closed the door, and went directly into his dining room where he kept his alcohol. He poured himself a generous serving of scotch and downed it in one gulp. The burn felt so good as it worked down his throat that he poured himself another, though he intended to sip this one.

He went into the living room and plopped down on the couch before setting his drink on the table. He shifted so he could work his cell phone out of his pocket and made a call. When he could tell it connected, he didn't waste time with pleasantries. "A little bit of a warning would have been nice, you fucker."

"I wasn't sure you'd man up and go talk to her if I told you it was her."

"Are you questioning my manliness?"

"Yes," Jace replied simply.

"Good call. I may have hidden in my house if you'd told me."

"See how well I know you?" Jace teased. "So how'd it go?" Jace asked after a beat of silence.

"Fine."

"Gabriel," Jace warned.

"What? It was fine. It wasn't at all painful to see the woman who stomped on my heart."

"What'd she say?"

"That she was sorry. That she was glad to have known me even though it all went to shit. You know, the usual."

"You don't have to do this whole nonchalant thing with me. We can have a real conversation."

"We've had too many of those recently. I'm past my quota."

"You going to see her again?"

Gabe snorted. "Why the hell would I do that? She came here for closure, and I gave it to her. There's no reason to keep in touch."

"No reason other than you're madly in love with her."

"I'm in love with who I thought she was. I don't even know the real Rachel."

"Do you really believe that?" Jace asked as if he truly wanted to know.

Gabe lowered his head to his hand and groaned. "I don't know, man. There's no way to know. I can't deal with that kind of doubt."

"Okay."

"Okay?" Gabe was surprised by the easy acquiescence of his best friend.

"Yeah. Okay. You're the only one who knows what you can and can't handle. It's not my place to question your limits."

"Wow. Cool. Thanks."

"If I *were* someone who questioned those things, I might say that you're probably the strongest guy I know, and that there's nothing I don't think you can overcome if you want it badly enough. But I'm not that type of person, so I'll let it go."

"You're as subtle as a tire iron to the face," Gabe muttered.

Jace laughed. "Seriously though, dude. Look into your crystal ball and see which option seems like it'll suck less: being with her or without her."

Throwing his free hand up, Gabe exclaimed, "I don't know which will suck less! Everything is all messed up in my brain." Gabe took a second to calm down. "She broke my heart, Jace. I don't know how to get past that."

"Then I guess without her it is."

"Yeah. I guess."

"You want me to come over? Hang out for a while?"

Gabe rubbed his hand over his face and stood up. "Nah, I need to be alone and decompress. Thanks for the offer though."

"Anytime. I'll talk to you later."

"Later." Gabe ended the call and tossed his phone onto the couch. He wandered around his condo, trying to find something that would keep him occupied, but nothing held any kind of appeal. He wanted to be mad at Rachel. He'd been starting to heal until she'd shown up and reopened the wound.

But he couldn't be. Not really. He hadn't been mad for a while. Hurt, sure. But his anger... that had faded almost as quickly as it had come. The loss he'd felt after she'd left was greater than any other emotion he could muster, until eventually they all dwindled down to nothing. All that was left now was the profound sadness that came when you no longer had the thing that was most important to you.

Because even though that thing was close—only three blocks away, in fact—the divide between them seemed insurmountable. Gabe had beaten a lot of odds in his life. But he had no idea how to beat this one.

He walked over to the window and thought. For the first time since it first happened, he allowed himself to think about all of it. To let the memories flood through him and decide if he felt they were real or a trick. Then he tried to do what Jace had asked of him: decide which version of the future would suck less.

RACHEL

Rachel had taken her time getting back to her hotel. She briefly entertained the idea of stopping and grabbing dinner at the hotel restaurant, but she wasn't very hungry. If she wanted something later, she'd order room service.

Once up in her room, she changed into workout clothes, not because she was going to work out, but because she wanted to lounge around in something that didn't have an inflexible waistband. She threw on a pink tank top, sans bra, and grabbed the remote in hopes of finding something mindless to watch. She was on her second rotation of channels when there was a knock on her door.

She narrowed her eyes in confusion before going over to check the peephole. When she looked out, she was only further confused, but she quickly opened the door nonetheless.

The sight that greeted her made her eyes water for the second time that day. She was clearly becoming emotionally unhinged, though she wouldn't have changed a single thing about it even if she could. "Gabe," she whispered almost reverently.

He settled his hands on both sides of the doorjamb, his

eyes boring into her. "Which would suck less: life with me or without me?"

"Is that really a question? Life without you is unbearable." The tears streaked down her cheeks. She didn't even try to wipe them away.

"I thought so, too," he said.

"I don't—"

Her thought was cut off by Gabe stepping into her space and burying his hand in the hair at the back of her neck. "I don't know what I'm doing here, Rach. But I do know that there's nowhere else I'd rather be. I can't imagine living the rest of my life without you in it." He caressed her cheek with his thumb. "I already gave up one thing I wasn't ready to lose. I don't want to make the same mistake again."

With that, he tilted her chin toward him and kissed her. It was a slow, sensual, meaningful kiss that warmed her all the way to her toes. Filled her to the brim with so many good emotions, she was worried she'd float away on the lightness of it all. If she was ever to have a perfect moment, she knew that this was it.

She allowed herself to get lost in this experience that she never thought she'd have again. Clutching at him, she pulled him into the room. She barely registered the door closing behind him as she lost herself in the kiss, the feel of his hands on her, and press of his solid body. It was euphoric.

He steered her backward, and she broke the kiss to say, "So this is real then? You're sure? You have to be sure. I couldn't take it if you changed your mind."

"I'm sure," he said as he nibbled her neck. "I want you. This. Us. Forever."

Her hands found both sides of his face as she pressed

her lips back to his. When the backs of her legs hit the bed, she lay back on it. Gabe followed closely behind, pausing only to remove his shirt before he settled between her thighs. She tilted her pelvis up so she could rub against the hard ridge in his jeans.

"Somebody missed me bad," Gabe said with a laugh.

"You have no idea."

He let his fingers caress her cheek. "I think I do." He dipped to kiss her again, pulling away only long enough to take off her tank top. His hands immediately found her breasts and toyed with the nipples. "No bra. It's like you were expecting me."

His tone was light. Joking. But she wondered if on some level she hadn't been hoping this would be the direction this night would go—no matter how unlikely the possibility was to her. "If I'd have known that's all it took to get you here, I would've gone without for the past three months."

He laughed softly before looking deeply into her eyes. "I missed you," he said quietly.

"I missed you, too."

And then the time for words was over. Gabe stood to pull off her pants and panties before pulling a condom out of his wallet and stripping off the rest of his clothes. He didn't waste time rolling the condom down his hard length and positioning himself on top of her.

He reached down with one hand and caressed her clit, then shifted his fingers back farther and pushed them inside of her. Bringing his fingers up to his mouth, he licked them clean. It was filthy and erotic and the hottest thing she'd ever seen— aside from Gabe himself.

A long, breathy moan escaped her when he pushed inside,

stretching her in delicious ways. She felt every groove of him as he slid along her inner walls. He pumped into her with an urgency that demonstrated the frenzy of emotions that were swirling between them.

What existed in that room was both too much and not enough.

She arched her back in ecstasy as his fingers dipped back down to her clit and rubbed soft, steady circles that drove her to the brink of madness but not quite tipping her over the edge.

His thrusts moved faster as his pants became harsher. They were both balancing on a precipice. Together. Hopefully, *always* together.

He lowered his head to her nipple and sucked. That combined with the ministrations of his fingers and the pounding of his cock caused her to tumble into her orgasm, her entire body seizing as if a lightning bolt had shot down her spine.

Gabe continued to pump into her, his strokes becoming choppy and stilted until he stalled completely, throwing back his head, and pulsed inside of her. Then he made a few more shallow thrusts that caused his body to quake. When he stilled, he lowered his body so that the full expanse of their skin was touching.

"I love you," he said with a sweet smile.

"Love you back. Always." The words were more than a declaration.

They were a promise.

CHAPTER THIRTY

GABE

"I feel like this is a mistake," Gabe said as he held the door open for Rachel. He felt the sweat on his palms against the metal door handle.

"Why? It's all you've talked about for the last two weeks."

"Yeah, but it's one thing to talk about it. It's another to have to actually go through with it."

Rachel rubbed his arm as they approached the front desk. The woman sitting there had them sign in and, after asking a few questions, directed them to a small waiting room while she went to retrieve the person who would help them.

Gabe and Rachel took a seat as they waited. It wasn't until Rachel put a hand on his knee that he realized his leg was jumping.

"You're being ridiculous," she said with a slight laugh.

"This is a big moment for me," Gabe defended.

Rachel gave him a placating tap. "I know."

"I don't think you realize how big of a deal this is. It's not every day a guy becomes a father."

"I know. I'm sorry. I'm not trying to—"

Her words were cut off by a door swinging open. "Here he

is," Micah crowed as he walked toward them.

Gabe's eyes shot toward the voice before drifting lower to the beautiful creature next to him. In that moment, all his nerves and reservations melted away. He sank to the ground beside the bench he'd been sitting on and held out his hands. "Hiya, buddy."

Not even a second later, Gabe's arms were full of excited, wriggling fur. A giant tongue came out to bathe his face.

Rachel and Gabe had gone back to the shelter a few times since they'd gotten back together. With Rachel able to work remotely most of the time, she'd been spending considerable time at Gabe's place in Philadelphia. After about a week of them mostly hanging around the house, Rachel decided they needed a project.

To Gabe's chagrin, that project was helping him get over his fear of dogs. Gabe had tried to talk her out of it, but she'd become fixated on the idea, so back they went to the shelter.

Gabe had originally thought Micah was fucking with him when he had him spend more time with Torque, but it ended up being a blessing in disguise. Once Gabe got over being nervous around the gigantic animal, Torque also relaxed. Not long after that—during dinner when Gabe was recounting his day with Torque even though Rachel had been there—she suggested that he just adopt the dog he was clearly in love with. Gabe had played it off by asking if Rachel was jealous, to which she shot him the finger, but the seed had been planted.

And now here they were, ready to adopt Torque and take him home. Thank God he was good with cats, since those little assholes had grown on him as well.

Micah handed over the lead, gave some last-minute instructions, and wished them all the best. It nearly killed Gabe to crate Torque for the ride home, but Micah and Rachel had both insisted that it was the safest way for him to travel. Once home, Gabe hopped out of his SUV and practically sprinted to let the dog out. "Come on, buddy. I'm sorry I had to lock you in that prison. The mean lady made me."

Rachel shot him a dry look that made Gabe laugh. They led Torque around the small patch of grass on the side of Gabe's building so he could sniff around and do his business. Then they walked him to Gabe's condo.

Rachel hurried in front of them and started to unlock the door with the key Gabe had given her. She gave him a small smile before throwing the door open.

Gabe heard a loud, "Surprise!" before his eyes processed what he was seeing. Ben, Ryan, Jace, Aly, and some of his other close friends were all standing in his house wearing party hats with dog ears hanging from them. The living room had been decorated with streamers and balloons, most of which said "Congratulations" or "It's A Boy."

"You guys look like assholes," Gabe said, but a laugh soon followed. Because really, who wouldn't be touched by a surprise party for a dog?

"That's good, because we feel like them too," Ben said as he slid his hat off his head.

Everyone laughed and then walked over and greeted Torque. Torque was uncharacteristically shy at first, choosing to stay close to Gabe, but he eventually loosened up. Especially when Rachel brought out the cake she'd had made at a doggy bakery she'd found a few blocks from their place.

As his friends milled around and talked, Gabe sidled up to Rachel and put an arm around her shoulders. "Thanks for this," he said as he placed a kiss on her temple.

She melted into him. "Of course. It's not every day the love of my life becomes a daddy to someone else's offspring."

Gabe chuckled but then pulled her even closer. "Maybe someday I'll be a daddy to your offspring too."

Rachel turned her head and looked deeply into Gabe's eyes. A slow smile spread over her gorgeous face. "Sounds like a plan."

EPILOGUE

GABE

Two years later...

"This is the life," Gabe said on a sigh as he relaxed back into the hammock.

Rachel snuggled into him, the sides of the hammock causing her to be practically on top of him. "It is. We should get one of these things."

"And put it where?"

"We can figure out a way to hang it on the balcony." Rachel rested her head on his chest.

Since Gabe was down for any plan that put Rachel in his lap, he said, "Okay. We'll figure it out when we get home."

Rachel turned her head up toward him, and Gabe was just about to press a kiss to her lips when he heard a loud voice.

"I can't take any more heterosexual affection this weekend. Please. Just stop."

Gabe smirked at Camille. "You're the one who brought a guy as your date to this thing."

Ben, who walked out onto the long wood porch behind Camille, said, "Thanks for referring to my wedding as 'this thing.' Some best man you are."

Gabe shrugged. "Don't hassle me. I'm finally enjoying myself."

Ben let out a laugh. "You're such a dick."

Gabe laughed too. The truth was, the events Ben and Ryan had planned for the week leading up to their wedding had been pretty fun, but Gabe wasn't going to let him know it. He'd initially balked at having to spend an entire week doing wedding activities, but it had been important to the couple. "I'll just be glad when you guys are married so you'll stop having to prove how much better you've gotten at party games."

"We will never have to stop proving that," Ben said seriously.

Gabe chuckled again. "Well, for both your sakes, you may want to stop anyway. The two of you still suck at them." Gabe could just make out Ben's glare in the soft light that filtered from the lanterns lining the porch and the small bit of sunlight that hadn't fully disappeared over the horizon. "Where is the bride-to-be anyway?"

"I don't know. She was right behind me," Ben said as he moved back toward the door that led inside the enormous and extravagant cabin Ben had rented out for them for the week before his wedding. Just as he reached the door, it abruptly swung toward him, not giving him time to grab it. The wood smacked him in the face, causing him to immediately double over.

Gabe jumped up and rushed over to Ben, moving him back gently so he was out of the door's path.

"Oh my God, what happened?" Ryan said, her voice laced with alarm.

Ben straightened, but his hands still cupped his nose.

Ryan took one look at him and burst out laughing. "Oh shit. This is perfect."

"I fail to see the humor," Ben replied, even though there was a hint of amusement in his voice.

"I hit you with a door," Ryan said through her laughter.

Ben dropped his hands. He had a welt already forming from the bridge of his nose to his hairline, but he was smiling.

Gabe couldn't get over how fucking nuts his friends were.

Ryan moved forward and slid her arms around Ben's neck. "It's like coming full circle. We really are meant to be together."

Ben put his hands on her hips. "Were you doubting that?"

"No. But it's nice to have a sign." Ryan pushed up onto her tiptoes as Ben lowered his head.

Camille took a step toward them. "That's going to—"

Ben groaned when their noses pressed together as they kissed.

"Hurt," Camille finished.

Jace and Aly approached the porch hand-in-hand. They'd gone to the main part of the hotel to call home since the reception was better there and they wanted to Facetime the twins, who were staying with her parents. The twins had just turned a year old, and Jace had practically had to drag Aly away for them. They'd opted not to come for the whole week and instead had just flown into Colorado that morning and were leaving the day after the wedding.

"How are Gabe and Gabrielle doing?" Gabe asked them.

"I don't know who those people are, but Justin and Bella are fine," Jace answered.

Gabe sighed loudly. "One day, you'll smarten up and accept their true names."

Aly laughed as Jace walked up onto the porch and shoved Gabe. "Save those names for your own kids."

Gabe's eyes widened as he jerked his head to where

Rachel was sitting up in the hammock. "Ixnay on the babay-ay... How the fuck does pig latin work?"

"Smooth, Gabe," Ben joked.

Gabe looked over at Rachel and their eyes locked. The slight quirk of her lips told him she knew what his words were: a joke. They'd been talking about the possibility of kids for a while, and Gabe had considerably warmed to the idea. Still, "Let me tackle one major life change at a time. I still have to convince her to not stand me up at the altar in two months."

Everyone looked over at Rachel, who merely said, "I can't make any promises."

Gabe sighed heavily as if he were extremely put out before turning to Camille. "If she bolts, you're going to have to step up and take one for the team."

"You mean by going after her and convincing her to give me a shot? Because that's what *my* team would want me to do."

"You're so selfish. Where's your date anyway?"

Rolling her eyes, Camille said, "Kellan isn't my date. He's my escort for the week."

At her words, everyone's gaze swung to Ryan. "Nice," Ryan muttered.

"Don't worry. I'm not the kind that puts out. At least not for chicks," Kellan announced as he walked out onto the porch. He watched Ben rub his hand over his nose, and said, "What the hell did I miss? Is this some weird straight-guy athlete thing? Do we all get to punch him in the face?"

"Ryan hit him with the door," Camille explained.

"On purpose?" Jace asked, genuine curiosity evident in his tone.

"No, asshole," Ben groused.

"Let me take a look," Aly said as she moved toward him.

"I'm fine," Ben said, even though he willingly let Aly lead him closer to the light so she could inspect him.

"Shut up and let me look," Aly said, her doctor voice making an appearance.

"What time do we have to meet your family for dinner?" Gabe asked Ben.

"In about forty-five minutes," he answered before hissing as Aly pushed on his nose.

"It's not broken, but that welt is going to look fantastic in your wedding pictures tomorrow."

"I've survived worse," Ben said as he stood up straight.

Ryan moved to him and put her arm around his waist. "It'll give the pictures character."

"There will already be a character in them. Gabe will be there," Jace teased.

"Your jokes have taken a turn for the worse since you became a father. You better hope that one doesn't take the remaining shreds," Gabe joked as he pointed to Aly's stomach.

Jace glared at him, and it took Gabe a second to realize why. "Fuck."

Aly walked over and smacked Jace on the arm. "I thought we were waiting to tell people until after Ben's and Ryan's wedding."

"I had to tell someone. It's not my fault he's a moron," Jace argued.

"You've known me my entire adult life. If you haven't learned by now that I can't keep a secret, then who's the real moron here?" Gabe asked.

There was a flurry of activity after that. Everyone rushed toward Aly to hug her and wish them congratulations. Gabe stood off to the side, surveying the scene. He was going to have that one day: everyone wishing him well because he was having a baby with an incredible woman. And he wasn't going to have Gabe Jr. with just any incredible woman, but the beautiful one whose soft brown hair fanned out over her shoulder as she turned to seek him out in the small crowd. Gabe was really a lucky son of a bitch.

Rachel walked over to him and right into his arms. They held one another as they gazed lovingly into each other's eyes. "You really do have a big mouth," she whispered.

Gabe ducked his head down so his lips were aligned with hers. "The better to kiss you with." And with that, he ghosted his lips over hers.

The kiss consumed him, as it always did whenever his lips touched hers. But it was also more. It was a pact. A promise. That this was just the first step of many for them. That this relationship that was born out of a one-night stand would go on to withstand the test of time.

ACKNOWLEDGMENTS

We have to start with everyone at the Nancy Yost Literary Agency, from the interns who read this over and over again to Natanya, who changed the cover multiple times until we thought it was perfect. And, of course, last but certainly not least, thank you to our fabulous, sassy southern agent, Sarah Younger, for helping us fit all the pieces together so we could get this book out to the world as soon as possible.

To our Padded Roomers, thank you for staying with us. We promise to post more! We swear!

To Erik, Mya, and Mason: Thank you for all the love you give me every day. You inspire me to push myself beyond what I ever thought was possible.

To Nick and Nolan: I couldn't love two guys more than I love the two of you. Nick, you're the best daddy, husband, and friend, and I love you more each day. Nolan, thank you for finally understanding that writing is one of Mommy's jobs and for letting me open a computer next to you without smashing all the keys.

ALSO BY ELIZABETH HAYLEY

The Love Game:
Never Have You Ever
Truth or Dare You
Two Truths & a Lime
Ready or Not
Let's Not & Say We Did
Tag, We're It

Love Lessons:
Pieces of Perfect
Picking Up the Pieces
Perfectly Ever After

Sex Snob
(A Love Lessons Novel)

Misadventures:
Misadventures with My Roommate
Misadventures with a Country Boy
Misadventures in a Threesome
Misadventures with a Twin
Misadventures with a Sexpert

ABOUT ELIZABETH HAYLEY

Elizabeth Hayley is actually "Elizabeth" and "Hayley," two friends who love reading romance novels to obsessive levels. This mutual love prompted them to put their English degrees to good use by penning their own. The product is *Pieces of Perfect*, their debut novel. They learned a ton about one another through the process, like how they clearly share a brain and have a persistent need to text each other constantly (much to their husbands' chagrin).

They live with their husbands and kids in a Philadelphia suburb. Thankfully, their children are still too young to read their books.

Visit them at AuthorElizabethHayley.com

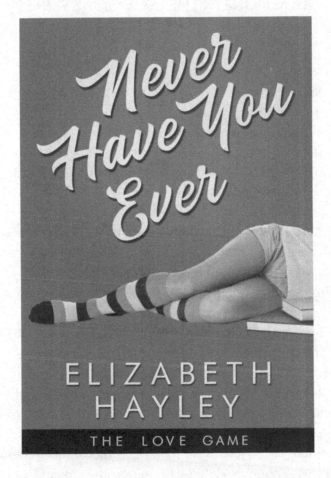

EXCERPT FROM

NEVER HAVE YOU EVER

BOOK ONE IN THE LOVE GAME SERIES

"Sophia Mason, you are here in the presence of your sisters to atone for your sins."

"I think 'sins' is a little extreme, Aamee," someone said.

It might have been Gina, but I couldn't be sure. I couldn't see anything in the dark room except the blinding flashlight of Aamee's iPhone shining in my face.

"Shut up, Gina," someone confirmed.

Aamee got closer to me, bringing the light with her. It was like I was heading toward my inevitable death, but instead of feeling a peaceful calm as I sat surrounded by loved ones, I was battling a power-hungry college senior who was permanently PMSing.

I moved back and turned my head to the side so the light wasn't directly in my eyes. "Can we turn that thing off and have a normal conversation about this, please?"

There was silence for a few moments until the light shut off and a lamp turned on instead. "Fine," Aamee said, "but the process is still the same."

Some of the girls were looking at their nails in between eye rolls, seemingly siding with me on the ridiculousness of this. Others were nodding as Aamee spoke, though I wasn't sure if it was because they agreed with her or were just too scared *not* to.

"Can we just get this over with?" I asked.

I knew Aamee was pissed about Carter, but after my conversation with Gina, I'd let myself get my hopes up that my punishment began and ended with her silence toward me over the past two days. It was a consequence I was happy to accept since it was more of a reward than a punishment.

Aamee flipped her blond hair behind her shoulder and pursed her red lips together. They were so plump, I'd once asked if she'd done "whatever Kylie Jenner had done." I'd quickly identified that question as a mistake, but it was too late to take it back. And thus began her hatred of me.

That night she'd announced the addition of my name to her Shit List, and I'd only moved up in rank since then by doing little things like using her toothpaste or disconnecting her phone from a charger so I could charge my own.

"Then let us begin," Aamee said. "On the fifteenth of September, you, Sophia Marie Mason—"

"My middle name isn't Marie."

"Sophia Elizabeth—"

"Nope."

"Ann?"

I shook my head.

"Whatever. Like…ninety percent of the female population has one of those. I just guessed."

"Well, you guessed wrong."

"Do you plan to tell me what it is?"

I pretended to think for a second. "No, I think I'll leave you in suspense."

Aamee composed herself, though she looked like she was ready to explode. Which, after picturing it, I realized would've been amazing to watch. Long strands of yellow hair painted red from her blood, her spray-tanned orange skin splattered all over the walls like some sort of abstract painting.

Unfortunately, my Aamee fantasy was interrupted by her voice. "On the fifteenth of September, you, Sophia—"

"You should probably include the year," Gina said, sounding like she was choking back a laugh. "I mean, if we're being formal about all this."

Aamee's lips looked like they were ready to pop when she pressed them together. "Any other requests?" She looked around the room.

"You do you, sweetie," Bethany shouted. "You're doing great."

"On the fifteenth of September, you, Sophia . . . Something Mason, were caught harboring a male student in your room during nighttime hours."

My eyebrows raised. "Harboring? Really? You make him sound like a fugitive."

"That's enough of the interruptions. May I continue?"

I gestured with my hand, though I knew I didn't exactly have a choice.

"According to the Zeta Eta Chi handbook, which our founding sisters created at the induction of this chapter, and I quote, 'No male shall be permitted to spend more than four consecutive hours in the house, and those hours must not be between dusk and dawn for the sole purpose of preserving the organization's reputation of integrity, honor, and respect. Any member found to have disobeyed this regulation shall, at the sole request of the chapter president, be evicted from the house immediately.'"

Aamee closed the book and waited for a reaction. I didn't give her one.

"You're citing a manual from almost a hundred years ago."

"The age is irrelevant. What matters is the content. Do you dispute the fact that a male was in your room overnight?"

"No. Do you dispute that one was in yours a few weeks ago?"

Aamee appeared flustered for a moment but regained her composure quickly. "Good thing I'm the president."

"Way to abuse your power. You're really going to kick me out of the house for this?"

"Punishment fits the crime if you ask me. If you can't abide by house rules, you can't live in the house."

"Oh, come on. Let's call it like it is. You're pointing a finger at me because the 'male' who stayed over is someone you have a major crush on. And while a big part of me wants to lie and say I slept with him so I could watch you raze this house like Carrie, the truth is all we did was fall asleep studying. So hop down off your moral high horse before you break your hypocritical neck."

She was eerily quiet, staring absently for so long it made me wonder if I'd put her into some sort of catatonic trance. It also made me wonder if my points had been valid enough to make her second-guess my punishment, though I doubted it. More likely, it was simply the calm before the storm. A few more seconds passed before Hurricane Aamee spoke.

"My decision stands. Don't do the crime if you can't do the time."

"Any more clichés you'd like to toss out? You're not going to tell me if I don't have anything nice to say, don't say anything at all?"

Aamee laughed. "Actually, I don't care what you have to say one way or the other. I just care that you leave."

This time it was Emma who came to my defense. "Aamee? You know Sophia's mom is Kate Macland, right? She was president. We can't kick Sophia out of the house."

"Of course I know who her mom is. How do you think she got in?" Aamee fixed her eyes on me. "Besides, it's not like she's out of the sorority completely . . . yet," she added with more hostility in her tone than had been there previously. "You should probably start packing your bags. You have twenty-four hours to get out."

"Thanks." I gave her a sickeningly sweet smile. "But I'll probably only need a few hours."

She laughed like I was kidding, but when I got all my stuff into boxes and suitcases with the help of Gina, Emma, and a few other girls who weren't attached to Aamee's tit—and left without making a big deal of it—I was certain Aamee's curiosity about where I'd gone might kill her. Too bad I wouldn't be there to see it.

I arrived at my brother's a half hour later with a hastily packed bag of clothes, shoes, toiletries, and various electronic gadgets. I hadn't called Brody to give him a heads-up, but our dad was paying for the place, so he couldn't exactly turn me away at the door.

We'd never been what I'd call close, but maybe we could be now that we were on the same campus and I'd be bunking with him—at least until I figured out how to get back into the sorority house.

Brody, a fifth-year senior, had been attending college halfway across the country—largely to get some space from our parents and me. But now, four and a half years and dozens of lost credits later, he was closer to home and trying to climb out of whatever hole he'd dug himself during his years of partying.

That our father had let him transfer again had been a shock to both of us. I'd thought for sure he'd make Brody throw in the towel and figure his shit out before he burned any more of his money at institutions of higher learning. But when Brody promised that a change of scenery and living by himself would help him focus, our dad agreed to give him one more shot before he pulled the plug on his education. I guess he had more faith in Brody than the rest of us did. Brody included.

It occurred to me, as I shifted my bags at the door of Brody's apartment situated above a small bakery, that I should've at least checked to see if he was even going to be home. For all I knew, I could be spending the next five hours waiting for him to get back from class.

Thankfully someone opened the door when I knocked. Instead of my shit-for-brains brother greeting me, it was a handsome stranger.

Guess my brother had already made some friends. Hot ones.

"Hi, I'm looking for Brody. Is he here?"

The guy opened his arms wide and plastered on a smile. "You found him."

What?

"I'm sorry, is Brody here?"

"I'm Brody. Can I help you with something?"

"You're not Brody."

He jerked his head back like the accusation was absurd, and for a brief second, I wondered if I'd somehow entered the Upside Down and was in some sort of parallel universe where nothing made sense and my brother was a gorgeous stranger who looked happy to see me.

I pushed past him without waiting for an invitation. "Brody! Brody!" I called as I moved through the apartment.

"I'm right here. I'm sorry, *who* are you?"

"The better question is who the hell are you? Because I'm Brody's sister, and you're sure as shit not Brody."

The story continues in...

Never Have You Ever

Available Now!